THE RADIO GUN-RUNNERS

Blood Ritual:
The Adventures of Scarlet and Bradshaw, Volume 1
BY THEODORE ROSCOE

Champion of Lost Causes
BY MAX BRAND

The City of Stolen Lives: The Adventures
of Peter the Brazen, Volume 1
BY LORING BRENT

The Complete Cabalistic Cases of Semi Dual,
the Occult Detector, Volume 2: 1912–13
BY J.U. GIESY AND JUNIUS B. SMITH

Doan and Carstairs: Their Complete Cases
BY NORBERT DAVIS

The King Who Came Back
BY FRED MacISAAC

The Scarlet Blade: The Rakehelly Adventures of
Cleve and d'Entreville, Volume 1
BY MURRAY R. MONTGOMERY

Sabotage
BY CLEVE F. ADAMS

South of Fifty-Three
BY JACK BECHDOLT

THE RADIO
GUN-RUNNERS

RALPH MILNE FARLEY

ALTUS PRESS
2016

EDITED AND DESIGNED BY
Matthew Moring

ASSOCIATE EDITOR
Ray Riethmeier

PUBLISHING HISTORY
"The Radio Gun-Runners" originally appeared in the February 22, and March 1, 8,
15, 22 & 29, 1930 issues of *Argosy* magazine (Vol. 210, No. 3–Vol. 211, No. 2).
Copyright © 1930 by The Frank A. Munsey Company. Copyright renewed ©
1957 and assigned to Steeger Properties, LLC. All rights reserved.
"About the Author" originally appeared in the February 22, 1930 issue of *Argosy*
magazine (Vol. 210, No. 3). Copyright © 1930 by The Frank A. Munsey
Company. Copyright renewed © 1957 and assigned to Steeger Properties, LLC.
All rights reserved.

ISBN
978-1-61827-233-1

Visit *altuspress.com* for more books like this.
Printed in the United States of America.

TABLE OF CONTENTS

CHAPTER I

HIJACKED

IT ALL HAPPENED absolutely without warning.

The seventy-five-foot motor yacht *Miami* was anchored not far from Belle Isle, off the Newfoundland coast. Her owner, Tom Jones, had just obtained his S.B., *summa cum laude,* from Harvard, and was taking a well-deserved summer rest, *en route* to visit some friends in Grenfell's colony in Labrador, before hanging out his shingle as a consulting engineer in the fall. At the moment, he sat in the shade of the pilot-house of his boat, with one of the crew, both fishing for tautog. The other member of the crew was polishing up the twin-six engines.

The navigator, Captain Antone Pease Ferreira, lay in the bunk room, dozing. Ferreira's sixteen-year-old tomboy daughter, who had come on the cruise with her father, was at the moment helping the Chink cook in the galley. The ship's cat lay in the sun on the deck. The Harvard Yacht Club flag flapped lazily at the masthead. All was blissfully peaceful.

The motor of another boat could be heard not far away. Then that sound ceased, and all was still again. There came a dull thump somewhere behind them, and the *Miami* trembled.

"Mike," announced the young owner of the *Miami,* "that sounds as though something bumped us. Will you go and see?"

Mike Murphy, a Cambridge cop whom Jones had laughingly invited to join his crew, arose, handed his fish-line to his employer, stretched himself, and ambled off around the pilot-house. Several minutes passed without his return, so Tom Jones finally hitched both lines to a cleat, and went to see what was keeping Mike.

As he rounded the pilot-house he was met by a strange young man holding an automatic as if he were quite used to doing so.

"Stick 'em up!" commanded the other, and Tom promptly obeyed. The hijacker, if such he was, had a rather likable face, now set in stern enough lines. He seemed about Tom's own age. He had wavy black hair, a small black mustache; his complexion was dark, but smooth and clear save for a long, rather distinguished-looking scar across his right cheek bone.

On one side of him stood a thickset, sinister, sour-visaged Italian. On the other side stood a small, middle-aged, wizened, horsy individual. All three looked like city gangsters to him.

MIKE MURPHY lay, bound and gagged, in the scuppers. Lashed to the rail was a craft slightly smaller than the *Miami*, and from it a villainous-looking crew were busily unloading packing boxes labeled "Canned Goods."

"What's the great idea?" Tom Jones demanded indignantly, but with his hands still held high.

"Our boat is leaking like a sieve, so we thought we'd change ships," succinctly replied the scar-faced man.

"Then why didn't you ask for help like a gentleman?" said Tom. "I'd gladly have given you a lift."

The only answer was a snort. Then, "Frisk him, boys."

In a few moments Tom Jones, bound and gagged, was lying beside Mike Murphy in the scuppers.

The unloading of the "canned goods" proceeded rapidly; then one of the intruders ran a fuse into the gas-tank of their deserted ship, lit the fuse, and cast their ship off, at the mercy of the strong tide. Several minutes later, after drifting quite a distance, it exploded with a dull *boom*.

The *Miami's* engines were started, and she headed out to sea. Scarface and the heavy Italian then returned to where Tom and Mike still lay bound.

The hijackers looked like city gangsters to him.

"Better bump 'em off, boss," the Italian was saying, as they approached.

"Too crude, Nick," replied the other. "We may need them to put up a front for us, if that British Navy boat that chased us in the Gulf of St. Lawrence ever gets on the trail again."

"Navy?" thought Tom to himself. "Since when has the British Navy been chasing rum-runners?"

Scarface continued, "We mustn't miss a single bet in getting these guns safely to Costa Rica."

So that was it? Gun-running, rather than rum-running. Filibusters, not bootleggers. Why, Tom thought, he might even consider joining in an expedition like this himself. Filibusters! Latin-American revolutions! Soft southern skies! Beautiful *señoritas!* Glamour! Intrigue! Excitement! What young college graduate would not take a flyer at some Richard Harding Davis filibustering?

He could not fail to observe that no one was offering him such a chance. He was no longer the rich owner of a palatial yacht; he was merely a prisoner of ruthless men who ignored him. He felt suddenly very small and unimportant.

The leader went on, "Untie the Chink and the cabin boy, and make them get us some grub, Nick. And send some one to stow these two in the bunk room."

And he strode forward to the pilot-house. Nick lumbered aft to the galley.

The mention of "cabin boy" brought the young college man to a sudden realization of Theresa Ferreira's predicament. Well, she would be as safe as the rest of them so long as these thugs thought her a boy. Lucky that she was wearing sailor breeches and a loose sailor blouse. With this costume and her boyish bob, it might be some time before this piratical gang found out her sex.

These thoughts were interrupted by the arrival of four burly members of the hijacking crew, who picked up the two bound captives and carried them below. As they passed through the mess-room, Tom saw the horsy little man twiddling with the controls of his nine-tube radio.

In the bunk room lay Captain Ferreira and Si Greene, the other member of Jones's crew, both bound and gagged. Tom and Mike were heaved unceremoniously into the bunks, and were left there, still tied.

An hour or so later food was brought them, and they were ungagged and partially unbound, so that they might eat. But the men who served them refused to answer any of their questions. After the meal, they were bound again.

Still later the Italian named Nick came, and asked them which was the engine-man. Informed that it was Si Greene, Nick released him and led him out. It seemed that one of the motors was behaving badly, and their own men couldn't fix it.

THE BOAT had begun to pitch and roll, indicating rough weather outside. Scarface came in, jauntily attired in one of Tom's own yachting costumes. He looked almost a gentleman in that outfit. The change in him was startling.

He untied Captain Ferreira. At this, his lieutenant, Nick, who had joined him, protested.

"Don't let too many of them loose, boss," said he.

"It looks like a storm," replied his chief, "and Little Arty has picked up by radio another Navy boat that's on our trail. We need an expert to run the *Miami* now."

"Don't say I didn't warn you," grumbled Nick, and then the two left with Ferreira.

How long the storm continued Tom never knew or cared. It could have been days or weeks. The *Miami* pitched and rolled. Tom, who had thought himself a sailor, was frightfully seasick and utterly indifferent to his surroundings.

When at last he came to, he found that he was no longer tied. Weakly he made his way on deck.

It was a strange and unexpected sight that met his eye. The *Miami* lay wedged in a floe of ice! And the air was bitterly cold.

Murphy came hobbling up, a pair of handcuffs on his ankles. They were his own handcuffs, mementos of the days when he had been a genial, hard-drinking Cambridge policeman and a favorite with Tom Jones's Harvard crowd.

"Where are we, Mike?" asked Tom, bewildered.

The Irishman scratched his head.

"I haven't been loose myself very long," he replied, "but as near as I can figure out, we've been blown way north in that divil of a storm, and are somewhere up near the top of Greenland. I heard Ferreira mention Smith's Sound."

Then the cold air drove them both below again.

In the mess-room Little Arty was tuning in Tom's radio set. Nick Fratelli was paging through a pile of Tom's magazines. Four tough-looking men of diversified nationality were playing poker with Tom's best pack of cards. Every one seemed perfectly at home. The owner of the *Miami* felt almost like an intruder on his own boat. He sat down heavily in a corner, and dully watched the game. Little Arty gave him a friendly grin, and Nick Fratelli glowered at him over his magazines, but no one else paid him the least attention.

Mike Murphy, his own man, came over and sat with him, and explained the situation briefly as follows: These men were part of the gang of Scarface Boston Jimmy. They had taken a contract to run a boatload of rifles and ammunition from Canada to Central America, but had been intercepted, driven off their course, and quite badly shot up when the naval patrol got wind of their scheme. So they had exchanged their own sinking ship for the *Miami*. But they had not dared buck that terrific storm, and now were lost somewhere in the frozen north.

Tom glanced around the room. The hijackers did not look particularly dangerous or vicious now; and Tom, who had been tensing himself for an instant clash, made up his mind to appear matter-of-fact and peaceful as he watched for an opening to turn the tables on his captors. Though there was little enough advantage to be gained now, imprisoned together in the ice as they all were.

Then Captain Ferreira came in.

"Well, well, well!" said the bluff old sea dog. "Glad to see you up again. We're stuck in the Arctic ice."

"So I see," replied Tom, a bit coldly. Then suddenly, "How's Terry?"

"He's all right," said her father, with the accent on the "he."

So their captors hadn't yet discovered Theresa's sex. Good!

That evening both crowds ate together. Ferreira, Terry, and Si Greene seemed quite at home among the intruders. Scarface was genial, though reserved. Only Nick Fratelli and one other—a bullet-headed Dutchman—remained sullenly aloof.

Then, because their clocks showed it to be nighttime, although the Arctic sun was still shining, they turned in. Tom slept in the bunk room with the crew, instead of in his own palatial stateroom, which had been usurped by the masterful Scarface.

THE NEXT day the ice began to loosen, but unfortunately it drifted north, carrying the *Miami* with it. The south wind stiffened. Antone Ferreira called all hands on deck, to fend off ice.

He was determined to make a frantic attempt to nose their way south through the drifting floe.

The Portuguese was in his element. He stood in the bow of the boat and took command. Scarface Boston Jimmy stood beside him, backing up the captain's authority. Tom Jones manned the wheel in the pilot-house, glad to have a hand in the running of his own boat once more. Si Greene tended the gasoline engines. The rest of the party were on deck, fending off the chunks of ice. Even Terry and Charley Loy, the Chinese cook, lent a hand. Every one helped except Tabby, the ship's cat.

Night came—that is to say, nighttime, for now they were at a latitude where the sun never set, at that season of the year, but merely circled the heavens, so night and day were divided off arbitrarily for them by the clock. It was time for them to turn in and rest, yet still they struggled on. The crew, enervated by seasickness and loafing, wanted to quit and call it a day, but Captain Ferreira insisted that it wasn't safe to quit.

However, he encouraged them with the prospect that the wind might die down at any moment and give them a chance to rest.

"If it doesn't," muttered Nick the Rat under his breath, "there's going to be trouble."

The crew groaned, grumbled, and finally threatened. The unfailing good humor and merry disposition of the supposed cabin boy kept up their spirits for a while, but at last even the effect of this lessened. Scarface cheered them on, and finally drove them with his dominating force.

But they were tired and cold. Although the sun did not set, yet it was very low. The sky was overcast, and the wind chill.

The sea was black and ominous. A dark fog arose, out of which fantastic white shapes of ice would suddenly ride into the beams of their searchlights and threaten to overwhelm them. The whole effect was ghastly.

Finally Nick Fratelli threw down his pole and announced defiantly, "I quit!"

Captain Ferreira was horrified. "Damn it, this is mutiny!"

"I think not," remarked Scarface quietly. "Nick, are you working or leaving the ship?"

There was no note of pleading in his tone, merely a calm assurance. A hush fell over the entire boat, as every one else stopped work and watched the two.

Nick stood, still defiant, hands on hips, facing his chief. Scarface stared back, a slightly amused smile on his lips.

Nick had crossed wills with his chief many times before, but never successfully. This time he was determined to make it stick.

Just then a huge piece of ice, the largest yet that night, loomed suddenly ahead, a bit to starboard. Ferreira shouted an order. Tom swung the wheel hard-a-starboard. But still the cake bore down on them.

"All hands ward off that iceberg," shouted Scarface Jimmy, and there was a general rush to the bow.

When the excitement was over, they noticed that Nick too was among them, holding his pole; it was the end of the mutiny.

IT WAS not long until Captain Ferreira announced, "Wind's dying down. It's likely to stop any moment now. Come on, boys, only a little more work to-night."

Encouraged by these words, all hands fell to and slaved like beavers. The *Miami* zigzagged ahead through the now almost stagnant but rapidly packing ice.

Presently Ferreira looked overside, stared aloft, and said, "Wind's down. All right, boys, we can't do any more to-night."

The ice was tightly packed around them again.

The order to go below was received with a weary cheer. But the rise in spirits was only momentary. They were all cold, exhausted, disgusted, their nerves at the breaking-point.

The next day was Friday, and there came staggering toward them across the ice a half-starved Eskimo. These two events may seem to have no connection with each other, but when they took the poor native aboard it led to their naming him— as had Robinson Crusoe—after the day on which he was found. They fed him and adopted him into the party, not alone from humanitarian motives, but likewise because his knowledge of Arctic life might come in handy. The dour and unfriendly Nick Fratelli even volunteered to teach him English.

SHORTLY thereafter a large crack developed in the ice. But the crack led only northward from there, and they wanted to go south. To the south was only unbroken ice.

Scarface, however, hated inaction.

"We'll go northward," said he. "I've heard that there's an open sea at the north pole. Perhaps we may be able to get out of that sea some other way."

Captain Ferreira assented, though for a different reason.

"We might even reach the pole," said he. "I used to dream of reaching the pole, when I was a boy on whaling voyages, but we never got even as far north as this."

"At least we won't meet any patrol boats up here," added Nick.

Soon the *Miami* was chugging northward.

Their progress was rapid—surprisingly so. The crack got wider and wider. But all this was leading them away from anywhere, into the unknown, and there were angry murmurs.

Then Scarface called them all together and made a startling announcement.

Said he, "I've been checking up on our speed and comparing it with the latitude readings which Captain Ferreira has been jotting down in the logbook."

"What's latitude?" asked the filibuster named Cicero.

"Aw, it's those lines on a map," snorted Little Arty.

Nick Fratelli glowered.

"Right, Arty," continued Scarface. "Well, those lines on the map mark off about seventy miles of distance to each degree of latitude, and our results don't check at all. We are making about twelve miles to a degree, instead of seventy."

"I've noticed that, and worried about it," interjected the ship captain.

"Well, don't worry any more," replied Scarface Boston Jimmy, with a reassuring smile, "for I've found the answer in a book."

"Nautical Almanac?" asked Ferreira hopefully.

"No. *Argosy*. I found some old copies in my cabin. There's a story I've been reading, about two young Milwaukee aviators who flew up to discover the north pole, and found a hole several hundred miles across, instead of a pole. The hole leads down into the center of the earth. The rapid curvature of the edge of that hole accounts for the fact that our latitude and our mileage don't check up. We think we are nearly at the pole, when really we're merely near the edge of that hole. See, here's a diagram of it in the magazine. That would explain it, wouldn't it, Jones?"

THE YOUNG Harvard man and several of the others crowded around to look at the picture. But most of the men were frankly uninterested.

Nick Fratelli smiled craftily to himself. In browsing through the magazines he too had run across this story, and had spelled out enough of it to form a theory as to where they were bound for. He had made some very definite plans for himself in this connection, but these plans he was keeping under his cap.

Tom Jones, in reply to their leader's question, reluctantly admitted that, if such an absurd state of affairs as a polar orifice were possible, it undoubtedly would explain the discrepancy between their mileage and their apparent latitude.

Then Scarface read to the crowd enough snatches from "The Radio Flyers" to give every one an idea of the author's theory of the polar hole, and the lost race of Vikings that inhabit the land inside the earth.

"Boys," he announced, "perhaps our getting blown north is going to let us in on a rich racket! I've a notion to try and go down through this hole in the top of the earth. There's enough rifles and ammunition to arm us all. The boat has its two machine guns, and most of us have gats. Listen to how the story ends."

Then he read:

"Here is the land of eternal warmth, where, the sun always shines. Here there is rich soil, big game, room for all. Here we have found power, adventure, happiness. We, Vikings, greet you of the outer wall. *Skaal!*"

But Tom Jones smiled a superior smile to himself. What gullible creatures these men were! He, as the only educated person in the party, knew that the story of the polar hole was mere absurd fiction.

All that day the *Miami* sped along. The wind was from the south, and the air was full of driving snow.

With the low hang of the sun, the clouded sky, and the thick drive of the snow, there was scarcely more light than at twilight back home, and what light there was had an ominous yellow-green color. Huge cakes of ice kept bobbing up unexpectedly to menace them, out of the wall of snowflakes which surrounded them. The searchlights were tried, but they only seemed to draw the wall closer, so they were shut off again.

Gradually the snowfall lessened. The obstructing ice cakes seemed farther and farther apart. Suddenly the sun shone upon them from dead ahead, the last flakes fluttered down, and in front of them was open water, stretching as far as the horizon.

The captain took a sextant-reading.

"Boys," he announced, "at this rate, we shall be at the pole in a few hours."

"Aw, forget it," sneered Nick Fratelli. "You guys read so much, and yet you can't remember for even a few hours that there ain't no north pole. Didn't the boss tell us that there ain't no pole? Even I have got that through my thick head."

"You're right, Nick," agreed Scarface, "both as to the pole and as to your head. There's nothing in either."

Nick Fratelli glowered.

As they sped along, the captain took frequent observations; and finally he announced: "We may not be at the north pole, but at least we're where the north pole would be if there were any such place. We're at 90° latitude."

A cheer went up from the crew, but Nick the Rat sneered again: "Aw, forget it. If they was any pole, it wouldn't be here. It would be 'way out ahead of us in the middle of the big hole we're bound for."

"Well, anyhow," commented Tom Jones, "if there is a pole, that's where we are now; and, if there isn't, we have an amazing adventure awaiting us inside the earth!"

CHAPTER II

DESCENT INTO THE UNKNOWN

THE *MIAMI* NOW proceeded to eat up latitude at a rate that would have indicated a perfectly phenomenal speed for the ship if the curvature of the earth, where they were, were such that some seventy miles equaled one degree, as would be the case in the inhabited portions of the globe.

Eighty-nine degrees, eighty-eight, eighty-seven, were successively indicated by the sextant.

A night shift was put at the wheel and the engine and the rest turned in.

When they awoke, it was noon. The captain estimated that they were well below eighty degrees, as the sun had set behind them.

"If we are still on the outer surface of the earth," said Ferreira hesitantly, "we'll strike Siberia to-morrow at this rate. But I'm beginning to believe the truth of that story which the boss read us."

The wind blew from dead ahead, and was quite warm.

By midnight, the sun was well up in the sky, and a sextant-reading showed that they had reached latitude 60°. In spite of the bright sun, the northern lights now showed brilliantly to the south of them.

"According to our clock," announced the Portuguese, "we are on the 120th meridian. At 60° north latitude, 120° east longitude, we ought, by rights just now, to be crossing southern Siberia, and about to enter Manchuria. And yet here it is open sea! Furthermore, we can't have come as far as thirty normal degrees of latitude in this short time. So I guess this cock-and-bull magazine yarn must be the truth, after all."

"According to our clocks it's midnight," remarked Murphy, "and yet look at the sun! And last noon, it was pitch dark. This has daylight saving beat a mile for complications!"

"But you forget," explained Captain Ferreira, "that we are on the other side of the earth now, where night is day and day is night."

"Then let's shift our clocks," suggested some one, "and start going to bed when it's dark and getting up when it's light."

"You forget," objected Scarface, "that we are not on the other side of the earth, at all. We are passing over the rim of the polar hole into the *center* of the earth. And, if the story is correct, it will soon be noon all day long every day."

"What I can't figure out," interjected Tom Jones, "is why the sun doesn't rise in the west and set in the east, now that we are inside the polar rim."

"It does," replied Ferreira.

"No such thing," exclaimed Tom, shocked out of his usual politeness. "Look here. When the sun rose, I faced north, and the sun rose on my right. Right hand is east, when you face north, isn't it?"

"Not when you've gone over the top and got inside the earth," explained the captain. "You see, when you're inside the earth, the sun rises in the west; but, as the west is now on the right-hand side of you when facing north, everything looks natural, just as before."

"It all depends on how you define 'east' and 'west,' doesn't it?" Tom objected, still unconvinced. "How would you define them?"

"**SUPPOSE** you had a pasteboard globe representing the earth," explained Ferreira, "the kind you get in school, you know."

"Yes?" said Tom, interestedly.

"Well, on the outside of the earth, 'east' means the direction toward which the surface of the earth is turning, doesn't it? Let's imagine you draw an arrow on the globe, representing east."

"Yes."

"Well, suppose you open up the globe to get a look at the inside of the pasteboard, which would represent where we are now, and suppose you draw an arrow on the inside, in exactly the same direction as the arrow on the outside, its head just under the head of the outside arrow, tail under tail. This inside arrow would point east, too, wouldn't it?"

"Yes, if it's drawn as you describe," Jones admitted.

Then triumphantly, "That inside arrow would point to the left of north; and so east is to the left of north inside the earth."

"Oh, I see," interjected Jimmy, with a snicker. "East is west and west is east, and never the twain shall meet."

"Not at all!" replied Ferreira testily, nettled by his chief's levity. "Here I get converted to your theory, and explain it logically, and then you go and make fun of it."

"Well, it's all clear as mud to me," asserted Little Arty. "Let's eat."

Sun setting in the morning, and rising in the evening. Sun setting in the east and rising in the west. East and west reversed from where they should be. It was all wrong!

"Fortunately this won't last long," said Tom, "or we'd go crazy."

The ship plowed on in darkness lit by the pink beams of the aurora borealis. And the location of the aurora was all wrong, too, lying south of them instead of north.

No stars showed in the southern part of the sky. It was as though a great bowl was gradually closing over the heavens from the south, slowly blotting the stars out with a distinct line of advance. And the edge of this bowl was faintly illumined, like the surface of the moon.

When next the sun rose, it rose from behind the rim of this bowl, rather than from the horizon. And then they observed what they had not noted before—that although there was a well-defined horizon ahead of them and behind them, which looked abnormally near, yet on each side of them the sea seemed to stretch away forever, curving up rather than down, until it merged into the sky in the distance.

Of course! To each side of them stretched the inside surface of the earth, curving ever upward; whereas behind and in front of them the water bent sharply across the edge of the polar rim.

By midnight, when the sun was almost overhead, their reading showed 25° latitude, and yet they knew that they were only a few miles inside the earth.

Soon the sun set behind the opposite edge of the rim, which by now had enveloped nearly half the sky. As they chugged on, they anxiously awaited its reappearance on their left, but it never reappeared. Instead, about fifteen hours later, a new and redder orb showed above the southern horizon, and rose slowly as they sped toward it.

"The central sun!" cried Jimmy.

Yet, in spite of their reading, it was hard to persuade some of them that they had not turned off their course; for a sun, by rights, ought to rise in the east or, at least, in the west, in this topsy-turvy world, rather than in the south.

Their gyro-compass, however, showed that they were still headed due south, and their gyro latitude-indicator appeared to show that they were a bit below the equator. Yet the climate was merely temperate; and whenever the wind blew from the north, quite chilly; in other words, like spring or fall in Massachusetts or Chicago.

LAND now appeared; many small islands among which the *Miami* threaded her way.

Some of the larger islands they explored, but found nothing of interest except some quite sizable rodents which they killed for meat. Tom was thrilled at this new world, of whose existence he had never dreamed, but this did not prevent him from keeping constantly on the alert for a chance to escape or regain control of the yacht. Scarface, however, never left Tom or any of Tom's former employees on the *Miami*, without making sure that they were outnumbered by fully-armed men of his own.

Scarface himself was as interested as Tom in this new world. So was Captain Antone Ferreira. But the rest of the party appeared either indifferent or bored. Nick Fratelli kept his views to himself.

One day they were resting after their return from an exploring expedition on shore. Arty was trying to get Sydney, Australia, his favorite station, on the air, with Friday as an attentive listener. But he didn't have any luck.

"It's no use," Arty asserted sadly. "Can't hardly get a thing now. Ever since we passed that place which Ferreira calls 90°, I've been having more trouble with the set. First all the little stations faded out. And then things kept on getting worse and worse, until to-day I can't tune in on even WEAF, KDKA or WLW. All I've got left now is WGY, I suppose on account of its extra-short wave."

"Ain't that awful!" snorted Nick the Rat, with mock sympathy. "What do you expect us to do about it? Weep?"

Arty gave him a black look, but said nothing. He was used to Nick's gibes at his interest in radio. Nick left the room.

The little ex-jockey continued twiddling the knobs. Scarface sat in his private cabin, reading. Charley Loy was in the galley. Nick Fratelli and little Terry were in the bunk room. The rest of the crew were variously employed, and all was quiet.

But things didn't stay quiet long. It was the lull before the storm. A loud commotion was heard in the bunk room, and then Nick rushed out, with his face streaming blood.

"That damn' little cat scratched me!" he snarled.

"Tabby?" asked Arty incredulously.

"Tabby, me eye!" replied Nick. "It was Terry Ferreira."

"Well," drawled Arty, "what were you doing to him?"

"Him?" exclaimed Nick scornfully; but just then the child burst through the door with cheeks aflame, and shouted: "You beast—I'll teach you to get fresh with me. Can't you leave a girl alone?"

"Girl?" gasped Arty.

"Sure she's a girl," grinned Nick, "and she's going to be my girl, too. I seen her first. But she's a young wild cat, and will have to be tamed."

"**YOUR** girl?" sneered Terry. "You dirty bum! I'd rather have even Charley Loy or Friday for my boy-friend than you."

"I'll teach you to talk back to me!" shouted Nick, advancing menacingly toward her.

"None of that, Rat!" snapped Arty. "Come on, Friday."

As the two leaped between Terry and her tormentor, a door at the other end of the mess-room opened.

"Well," said a calm and level voice, "what's the disturbance?" It was Scarface.

"Nick has insulted a lady, and so we was rescuing her," explained Arty.

"She's mine!" asserted Nick belligerently. "I seen her first."

"Lady? She?" inquired their chief in a bewildered voice.

"Me," said Terry, proud of being the cause of so much commotion.

Scarface advanced into the center of the room.

"You—a girl?" he asked.

"Sure," answered little Terry. "What did you think I was? Besides, no one ever asked you to take me on this trip; I was shanghaied. I never told you I wasn't a girl, did I? And this has all been such fun, until that beast started to get mushy."

"Well, I'll be—" began Arty, but words failed him.

"Then your name isn't Terry?" asked Scarface.

"Sure it is," she replied. "Theresa Ferreira. Terry, for short. But, Mr. Jimmy, you'll keep that wop away from me, won't you?"

"Keeping bums away from ladies is one of the easiest things I do," asserted Scarface. "You will occupy my stateroom."

"Ah," sneered Nick the Rat, "so you want her for yourself, do you? Well, I seen her first; and let me tell you, Scarface—"

He stopped abruptly. He was looking into the muzzle of an automatic.

CHAPTER III

EXPLORERS IN A WEIRD WORLD

"**NICK,**" **ASSERTED SCARFACE,** still covering the other with his gat, "you haven't even the first instincts of a gentleman, so I shan't bother to reply to your insinuations. Arty, will you go and tell this girl's father to stop the ship for a minute, and that I wish to see all hands in the mess-room? Miss Ferreira, please be seated."

"Gee," exclaimed Terry, slumping into a chair.

When all fourteen had gathered in the mess-room, Scarface returned his gun to his pocket, and addressed them:

"Little Terry Ferreira is a girl."

He paused for the import of this announcement to sink in. Captain Ferreira's face went ashy gray.

Scarface continued grandiloquently: "We are honored by the unsuspected presence of a lady on this trip, and must treat her with due respect. From now on, I shall bunk with the rest of you. Miss Theresa will occupy, alone and exclusively, what formerly was my stateroom. She is to be treated like a lady. If any member of this crew annoys her in the least way, there'll be one less of us. Is that understood? Then you may all go. Captain Ferreira, start up the ship again."

"Gee, Mr. Jimmy, but you're grand!" said Theresa admiringly. "To think what I've been missing all this while, by your not knowing I was a girl!"

The boat got under way again. Scarface moved his belongings into the bunk room, then went to the bow, where Captain

Ferreira was directing the navigation. Murphy was standing beside him.

"What time is it now, sir?" asked Mike, as he approached. "This is worse than daylight saving. There seems to be *nothing but* daylight up here. The sun stays in one spot in the sky, and it never gets to be any other time of day. This must be where they send all the daylight to, that they save up, back in the United States."

"I've always said," added Ferreira, "that if the Lord had wanted daylight saving, he would have made the clocks that way in the first place."

Scarface glanced at his wrist watch.

"It's 4 P.M.," he announced. "Time to change the watch; think I'll rearrange the shifts a bit. We must keep some one on guard all the while, for there's no telling when some strange creatures may attack us in this lost world, according to what we've read of it. Ferreira, you can have Arty, Si, Mike, George, Swede and Cicero. I'll sit up for another watch, and take the wheel. Scutari can run a gas-engine fairly well; he used to be a chauffeur. Nick the Rat can take your post. Tom and the Eskimo and your daughter can help watch for trouble. Let's go on farther inside the earth. If anything exciting happens, I'll call you."

Nick Fratelli was considerably mollified by being placed over Scarface, by Scarface himself. Also at having little Miss Terry in his shift. But he would have preferred to have had the latter pleasure, unadulterated by the former honor.

As they changed shifts, Antone Ferreira drew their leader aside.

"Sir," said he, "will you pardon me for suggesting, sir, that you're making a big mistake in trusting that Fratelli person? When he mutinied, back there in the ice, you'd ought to have put him in irons. Instead, you give him the run of the ship, and insult and trust him by turns. I can tell by the nasty look in his eye that he's just waiting for a chance to do you dirt."

"My dear captain," replied Scarface suavely, "you don't understand how to handle men. I've known Fratelli for years. I've managed him, and dozens of others like him. There's only one way to treat that type: trust them, and bully them, and make them like it. Then they will fear you and love you. That's the way Julius Cæsar used to do, and it's the secret of his and my success. Nick may bluster occasionally, and give me black looks, but he wouldn't dare try to 'do me dirt,' as you say."

As they separated, the navigator sadly shook his head, and muttered to himself: "Not merely dumb, as I had thought he was, but swell-headed. Oh, so swell-headed. It amounts to the same thing, in the end. I see trouble ahead for him—for all of us."

LATER that watch they were coasting some land on their right, when Scarface Jimmy suddenly exclaimed: "Look! See that crescent-shaped beach, with the cliffs behind it, and the woods on top? I'll bet that's where Eric Redmond first met the beautiful Viking girl. Remember about it in 'The Radio Flyers?' If so a path from the summit of the cliffs must lead to the plateau city, the northernmost outpost of Viking civilization. Let's land, and find out."

So the *Miami* swung her bow to starboard, and nosed gently in to the beach.

"It must be the place!" asserted Tom hopefully. By this time he had carefully read the story in question. "I believe that that long low rock to the right is the one that Eric hid behind, in his fight with the Eskimo-like natives, Skraelings."

Tom and Scarface had been navigating the ship together. They rushed on deck. The change in the course and the subsequent bump against the shore diverted the crew from their various preoccupations, and they now crowded out to see what was up.

Their leader ran his eye over them. Then he announced briskly:

"I want to tell you boys—and the young lady—that I think we have arrived at the landing-place of one of the cities of the Vikings. You all have read the story. Doesn't this look like the beach from which runs the path to the plateau, where Angus Selkirk rules as *yarl?* 'Beyond the Alps lies Italy.'"

"You don't mean to say that these are the Alps?" asked Nick Fratelli hopefully.

"Of course not, you dumb idiot!" scornfully replied Jimmy. "I was merely quoting some remarks that another great man— Napoleon—once made under similar circumstances."

"Well, try to keep down to earth as much as possible," grumbled the Italian. "We ain't all of us read books like you, you know."

Jimmy went on unabashed. "When I told you about the polar hole and my idea of hunting up a new racket down here, I didn't fully let you in on my plans. The world was invited here to colonize, but we have come here to stick up these squareheads. According to the story, there are only two civilized persons in this whole place, namely, the two Milwaukee boys, Eric Redmond and Angus Selkirk. Their plane is out of gas. Their rifles must be pretty near out of ammunition. We have plenty of both, and our gats and machine guns besides. With your help, I can put myself at the head of the government, make these Vikings fight for me, and conquer this whole new world. Stick to me, boys, and you'll all wear diamonds."

His announcement did not meet with the unanimity of approval that he had expected.

"Ay tank you ban make wan great mistake," enunciated Swede Johnson slowly. "T'ose Viking von't be so easy, I tank not."

"Do you call this exactly square?" added Tom Jones. "Two of your own fellow-countrymen come down here, win the love and affection of these people, and lead them to victory. Then they publish a general invitation to the U.S.A. to follow them and colonize. With the whole center of the earth open to you, do you call it exactly decent to pick on these two young men, and try to oust them from control, and enslave their people?"

"Jones!" snapped Jimmy, his scar showing dangerously red. "That will be just about all from you. You're not the chaplain of this trip."

Tom struggled to control his wrath, while Mike Murphy interposed his objection: "I don't know, chief. What's the use of shooting up some perfectly peaceful squareheads, when there seems to be plenty of land to go around, without doing that? I don't know."

"Murphy!" interrupted Jimmy, his scar still red. "When a policeman enlists under a gun-runner, he may expect to have to do things which do not exactly constitute preserving the peace. Any one else got any objections?"

Murphy, too, subsided, and the others hastened to register their approval.

"I SHALL take a small force, and reconnoiter," announced the masterful Scarface. "Murphy, Ferreira, Greene, Jones and Cicero. Nick, you are left in command in my absence. I wish you'd get busy teaching that Eskimo some English. You've been at it for days now, and we may need him at any moment as an interpreter to the savages here."

Nick Fratelli smiled a crafty smile to himself. He had purposely taught Friday little or no English. But he had managed to get Friday to teach him considerable of the Eskimo language—of which fact, however, no one else except Cicero had as yet any suspicion.

All hands turned in for a sleep.

After breakfast the next "morning," the members of the scouting party were each fitted out with rifle, automatic pistol, cartridge belt, and condensed rations.

Terry begged to be taken, but Jimmy told her: "I couldn't bear to risk your life."

She pouted and replied: "Gee, Mr. Scarface, does that mean that I'm going to miss all the fun of this trip? I wear boy's clothes still. Why can't you treat me as a boy again for a while?"

She begged so insistently that finally she was promised a place on the very next adventure.

Then the six pioneers set out. At the top of the cliff they found a path, as expected, and pressed on along it, uphill through the woods.

Nothing of moment happened, until about an hour later, when the bushes ahead of them at one side of the trail suddenly parted, and out stepped a gigantic black leopard, crouched low and tense.

The horrified explorers stopped dead in their tracks. Several started to draw their futile automatics—all the rifles were strapped across their backs—but Scarface signalled them down with a single peremptory gesture, for the beast was so near that to fire would be but to invite immediate and disastrous attack.

The leopard seemed intent on something across the path ahead of him. He stood motionless, except for his twitching tail, with his side toward them—the very picture of deadly feline grace and peril. They did not breathe as they stood motionless, and waited, too.

Finally, after what seemed ages, the head of the beast swung slowly around, until his yellow eyes regarded them squarely. The invaders wilted, unsure whether to stay "frozen" or make a frantic effort at defense or escape.

Then, as slowly, the leopard's head swung back to its original position, and it gave a tremendous bound, off the path into the tropical undergrowth. A moment or two later there came the death-scream of some smaller creature.

The six men unslung their rifles, and rushed past the haunted spot, and on up the mountain trail, as fast as their legs would carry them. After a run of several hundred yards, they paused, out of breath.

"You know," panted Cicero, "I prefer Chicago. It's a much safer place to live in. Look at the size of the black cat that just crossed our path!"

"And darn lucky for you that he crossed it, me lad," said Murphy, "instead of coming down it."

This quip somewhat restored the spirits of the party, and they started on again up the trail.

AT LAST, after many hours, they emerged upon open land, but it was not what they expected. Instead of a level plain they had read about, carpeted with red-pollinated flowers, and the massive cliff of the plateau rising in the distance, the field before them sloped sharply upward to a rugged and rocky mountaintop.

And when they reached the summit, there was no plateau to be seen ahead. Instead, the land sloped downward on all sides. The mountain on which they stood was the crowning eminence of a long peninsula. On three sides of them lay the island-dotted sea; while to the south there was a gradually descending ridge of lower peaks, and a widening of the land, which stretched off and up, without a break of sea, until it blended with the sky in the dim gray distance.

"Where's your Viking city, chief?" asked Murphy with a grin that took all the sting out of the taunt.

Tom was sincerely glad that they hadn't found it, with Scarface's racketeer intentions; but he hastened to console their leader.

"It would really have been too much to hope for," said he, "to have stumbled on the place right off the bat."

"Of course!" Ferreira suddenly interjected. "Eric and Angus went over the edge at longitude 30° off the northern tip of Greenland. We went over at longitude 60° up through Smith Sound. They headed due south. So did we. Our route must be about two hundred and fifty miles from theirs and rapidly diverging. We ought to head southwest to find them."

"Don't you mean southeast?" suggested Tom.

"Oh, hang this back-handed compass-system that they have down here!" snorted the ship-captain. "What I mean is, turn our bows to starboard. You can figure out the direction, and name it whatever you please."

"Look!" interrupted Cicero. "Isn't that an airplane off there to the south?"

All stared in the direction in which he was pointing. It certainly looked like a plane. And yet not quite.

"It must be one of those huge flying reptiles," asserted Scarface. "*Skwaas,* they call them. Bat-winged lizards seem to take the place of birds, when you get far enough into this country."

Then, for a while they stood in silence, taking in the view on all sides, while the motionless central sun beat down on them from exactly overhead. The rocks about them were covered with mosses and lichens. The sky was strangely off color, a dark and velvet blue, graying where it met the land or sea on every side.

It was easy enough to realize that they were inside a huge ball. In fact, the effect of blending of earth and sky made the ball seem infinitely smaller than it really was—gave them a sort of cooped-up feeling, hard to describe.

Turning their eyes to things nearer at hand, they scanned the dark green forests which surrounded them almost without a break.

"All this land will one day be covered by farms, and cities, and railroads, and concrete roads," exulted Scarface, but it was plain to see that he was talking more to himself than to his companions.

"Oughtn't we take possession in the name of the United States of America?" suggested Tom.

"No such thing!" retorted Scarface. Then, striking his foot on the rock, he declaimed: "I hereby take possession in the name of James Lefavour, alias Scarface Boston Jimmy."

"A lot of good it will do us, chief," Murphy cried out sharply. "There goes the *Miami,* leaving us high and dry in this God-forsaken spot!"

CHAPTER IV

STRANDED

"MAROONED!" YELLED ANTONE Ferreira with a curse. "The mutinous dogs!"

They all stared back in the direction from which they had ascended. True enough, the *Miami* was slipping steadily out into open water, bound a little to the left of south.

"What price empire now?" murmured Tom Jones to himself.

Cicero Tony Schultz also muttered something under his breath, cursing Nick Fratelli for leaving him in the lurch, when it was he who had first sowed the seeds of mutiny in Nick's brain.

"Come on!" shouted Scarface, and led the way back down over the rocks along the path up which they had come.

Panic-stricken, the others followed him. Never before had they realized what the *Miami* meant to them. With that boat, they were conquerors voyaging to subjugate new lands. Without the *Miami,* they were merely six city-bred men, unused to the woods, turned loose to shift for themselves in an unmapped and prehistoric wilderness, forced to learn its amazing ways before matches and ammunition gave out and clothing disintegrated. And even if they learned the ways of the woods in time to save their lives, nothing lay before them except a struggle for bare existence until old age finally conquered them one by one.

No wonder they raced madly, insanely, after the departing *Miami.* But by the time that they had covered the three or four miles to the shore, downhill though it was, the *Miami* was nowhere in sight. The six men collapsed panting on the top of the cliff which flanked the beach.

When they had rested for a while, they took stock of their provisions and other belongings. From one of his pockets Scarface produced a flash light.

"A lot of good that'll do us down here, where the sun never sets," remarked Tom Jones.

Its owner eyed him sharply.

"Never saw one of these before, did you?" he asked.

"Why, of course I have," laughed the one-time yachtsman.

"Oh, no, you haven't," asserted the other positively. "This is a signal-lamp, invented by our radio-hound, Little Arty. This little thing is a complete sending and receiving set. The case is wrapped with fine wire to serve as a coil antenna. Only half the inside is filled with batteries, and they are of a special kind, extra strong. The rest of the space is tube, and capacity, and a lot of other things I don't know the names of. But I do know how the thing works. When some one presses the button on one of them, the light flashes on the other."

Just then the light started flickering.

"Can you read Morse?" asked Scarface.

"Yes," replied Tom.

"Then listen in," Scarface ordered.

"Arty sending," came the message. "Nick has me trussed up in the cabin, but I got my hands on the light. The *Miami* went south only a little way. Nick is on a rampage, and there's hell to pay. Come—"

The message broke off abruptly.

"Look!" exclaimed some one, pointing down the beach to the southward.

All eyes followed the gesture, and saw a man trudging toward them, in what appeared to be civilized clothes which clung to his person as though wet. A series of yells of various sorts proceeded from the six on the cliff-top. The figure looked up and began to run toward them, while they in turn clambered down the face of the cliff and ran to meet him.

IT WAS Charley Loy, their slant-eyed cook, sopping wet and very woebegone. The six crowded around him and demanded an explanation.

"Dlunk," said he when he had caught his breath. "Nick Flatelli, he get into lum lockers. Dlink lotta lum. Get velly dlunk. Muchee whoopee. Thlow me overboard. Me walkee back flum lide."

Tom Jones was shocked at an abrupt thought that came to him. "Theresa is at the mercy of that crowd of drunken bums! We must rescue her. We thought we had only ourselves to save. But now we've got to save a lady."

"Lady, me eye!" snorted Cicero, still chafing under Nick's duplicity. "I should worry about a skirt!"

"No, you wouldn't," Tom snorted back at him.

"Do you mean to say," exclaimed Captain Ferreira, "that you'd all forgotten about my little Terry? Why, that's what worried me about the boat right along."

"This performance," stated Scarface levelly, "is going to be very bad luck for Nick the Rat. Charley, where was the *Miami* headed for, when you—ah—left the ship? And have you any idea where she is now?"

"Boat not go anywhere special," replied the cook. "Ev'lybody too dlunk. Boat just lun along shore, south. Nowhere particular."

"That fits in with Arty's radio message," Scarface said thoughtfully. "We'll follow the shore south."

Southward they tramped the sandy beach. How long, will never be known, for the sun hung always at noon above them, and no one thought to note the time by his watch. Occasionally they stopped to eat from the remainder of the rations which they carried, but there was no sunset to tell them when to sleep.

At last, when rounding the tip of a promontory of land, they saw the *Miami* drifting idly in a cove beyond. Before any one could hail her, Scarface had cautioned silence, and motioned his little band to take cover. But the precaution seemed needless. Not a soul was stirring on board. The boat appeared to be utterly deserted.

"Lord knows where they've all gone," exclaimed Scarface, "but at least we've got our ship back. How many of you can swim?"

Only Tom Jones and Si Greene admitted the accomplishment, so these two and their leader stripped, with the exception of belt and pistol, and waded out into the none-too-warm sea. The *Miami* was about a quarter of a mile distant, and drifting slowly away, under the influence of an offshore breeze.

"Lie low," was Jimmy's parting injunction to the four on shore. "But if any one appears on deck, then make a disturbance, and try to distract their attention from us."

"I wish I had got some of that rum," muttered Cicero Tony to himself. "If Nick ever gets another chance to make a break, I'm going to stick to him like a plaster."

ALL THREE of the men in the water were expert swimmers, and rapidly overhauled the *Miami*. Yet still there was no sign of life on board.

They had almost reached the boat when a shout from the shore caused them to pause and look around. Their first thought was that some one had appeared on deck, and that their four allies were attempting to create a diversion, as they had been instructed to do. But the decks were as deserted as before.

The commotion on the shore continued. The four men, standing on the beach, were pointing to the water to the south. The swimmers looked in that direction, and saw approaching them at a rapid rate what appeared to be a giant dolphin with alligator-like jaws. The nightmarish creature was leaping and diving, and weaving in and out of the surface of the water in its approach.

"An ichthyosaurus!" exclaimed Tom. "It comes from two Greek words—"

"Never mind where it comes from," interrupted Scarface. "It's coming toward us, and it looks hungry. I wish I could wake up from this— Come on, let's go."

And he began a frantic double-overhand toward the *Miami*, the two others needing no encouragement to make them follow at top speed.

Silas Greene was the least effective swimmer of the three. With appalling swiftness the sea beast bore down on poor Si, and cut him off from his two companions. He at once stopped swimming, and, treading water, drew his pistol and faced his assailant.

But at that very instant another beast of a different sort attacked him from the rear. A head like the dipper of a steam shovel, mounted on the end of a long, snake-like neck, suddenly shot out of the water behind him, and hung suspended over him. His friends gave a cry of warning. But even as he was turning to see what new menace was confronting him, the neck curved, and the head shot down upon him, enveloping the upper half of his body with its horrid jaws.

Jimmy's automatic barked twice. Two red spots appeared in the creature's neck, which gave a writhe as though in pain. At the same instant the other beast, cheated of its prey, hurled itself on the wounded reptile with a hiss of rage. The water, swirling in geysers, closed over the two beasts and their victim.

"He's done for!" gasped Tom.

Scarface was equally horrified. "If he's not, he'll certainly need our help when he comes to the top. Danger or not, we'll wait here till we see if there's any hope for him."

But nothing more was seen of either beast, nor of their prey.

" **SHAY**," inquired a thick voice out of the air above them, "did you shee what I shaw?"

Scarface whipped out his pistol again, and both men, treading water, looked up. The *Miami* had drifted almost upon them, and Scutari was leaning over the rail above them, beautifully drunk.

"Put up your water pishtolsh, an' come aboard," said Scutari genially. "Gran' little party!"

"Come on, Tom," said Scarface. "We can't do poor Si any good here, and we may possibly be able to help him from the *Miami*." Then to the surprisingly amiable drunk above them, "Lower us down a ladder, will you?"

"Shorry," replied Scutari, with a profound bow that nearly tumbled him over the rail. "No laddersh to-day. Thish' my day off."

So the two swimmers clambered up the side as best they could.

As Tom swung his last foot over the rail, the ichthyosaur rose in a graceful curve from the water behind him and snapped within an inch of his heel.

"A rotten miss," exclaimed Scutari. Then applauded feebly: "But it'sh the best show I've ever sheen."

Lying in the scuppers was the body of a man. Scarface turned it over with his foot. It was George, the Syrian.

"Dead?" asked Tom.

"Yes," replied his chief, "dead drunk." Then, to Scutari, "Where are the others?"

"Party in mesh-room," replied the Greek. "Shay, you'll get run in for indeshent exposure. Put on shum closhe. Haw, haw, haw!"

Scarface cuffed him into the scuppers alongside George. Then, brushing off his hands, he strode to the rail again for an anxious look at the spot where poor Si Greene had gone down. But the surface of the water was as calm and placid as though no tragedy had just been enacted there.

With a sigh Scarface turned away and entered the mess-room, followed by his aide.

The only occupants were Theresa and Nick the Rat. The two sat facing each other across the table. The girl was tied to her chair with many turns of rope. The bulky Italian sat at ease in his, with a half-filled glass and a bottle on the table before him. As the door crashed open, he was holding a table-knife by the blade, and was pointing at Theresa with the butt, evidently to emphasize something which he was saying.

As Scarface and Tom entered, Fratelli lumbered unsteadily to his feet and reached for one of his pockets. Instantly he thought better of it—he knew Scarface—and raised his hands aloft. Both of the intruders had drawn their automatics before entering.

"Quick, Tom, frisk him," ordered Scarface Jimmy. "And keep your own gun out of his reach while you do it."

Tom Jones walked over to the Italian and patted the latter's pockets, as he had often seen done in the movies. The patting having developed a lump in the right-hand coat pocket, Tom reached in and pulled out a gat, which he threw upon the table, as he had also seen done in the movies. Scarface hastily scooped up the gun and held it in his other hand.

"Nick, you big bum, you lousy double-crosser," growled Scarface, "sit down. Tom, untie Miss Ferreira, and tie up Nick."

Tom approached the captive.

But she expostulated, red-faced, and turning away her eyes, "Aw, gee, Mr. Jones, you and Mr. Jimmy haven't a stitch of clothes on."

SO INTENT had the two been on the developments since their return on board that they had completely forgotten their lack of attire.

Tom now promptly turned red himself and bolted for the door, only to be stopped by a peremptory, "Jones! There are two men still unaccounted for, and Little Arty's either locked up or knocked out somewhere. Never mind your modesty. Go and locate Swede Johnson and the Eskimo, and make sure that they are not in a position to cause us any trouble. And—and—" Scarface faltered, "you'd better bring me some clothes as soon as you've got those two birds disposed of."

Then his *sang-froid* returned, and he sat down, more or less shielded by the table from Theresa.

In a minute or two Tom Jones returned, clothed and bearing clothes. He untied the girl, and trussed up the Italian. Then Scarface Jimmy withdrew hastily and slipped into the garments which Tom had brought him.

On Scarface's return, his first inquiry concerned Swede and Friday.

"Both asleep in the bunk room," Tom reported.

"And now how are you, my dear?" Scarface asked, turning to Terry. "Did the Rat harm you?"

"Sure he did," replied the girl. "He bruised my arms up terribly with these ropes."

"Is that all?"

"Gee, ain't that enough?"

"Tell us what happened."

"Well," narrated Terry, "you see, after you had gone, the wop here he got nosing around all over the ship, and finally he let out a howl that he'd found a lot of booze. So everybody ran to see, except me and the Chink. The Chink shut himself up in the galley, and I tried to get on shore, but Scutari caught me and brought me back. The wop took me away from the Greek and locked me up in my own room—I mean your room, sir. I bolted the door on the inside, and then some one started up the boat. And they all drank a lot more, and sang and howled. And their the engines stopped, and no one seemed to care."

She paused for a moment, and then continued, "Well, after a while, I heard a splash and a lot of laughter, and I looked out the window—porthole, I mean—and the Chink was swimming away for dear life. They all tried to break down my door, but the wop came and cussed them something awful, so they stopped. Then the wop broke down the door himself, and wanted me to drink with him. So I slapped his face, and he tied me up and said he would teach me to be a lady. And then you came. And I guess that's about all, sir."

"It's quite enough," commented Scarface grimly.

"You poor little kid," said Tom Jones.

"**CAN YOU** handle a gun?" Scarface asked her.

"Gee, Mr. Jimmy," replied the girl, "you don't want for me to kill the wop, do you?"

"Not exactly," explained Scarface.

"That is, not unless it's necessary. I merely want you to keep him out of mischief, while Jones and I get this boat going."

So saying, he handed her one of the pistols. Grasping it in both hands, she placed its butt on the table and pointed the trembling muzzle at the bound man, who now turned pale for the first time.

"For Pete's sake, Jimmy," Nick begged hoarsely, "take her away! I can't stand to see that gat waving at me."

"Then shut your eyes, you fool," replied Scarface.

"That would be worse," moaned Fratelli, now completely unnerved. "It might go off without my knowing it. Take her away!"

"You've got it coming to you, Nick," asserted Scarface with a malicious smile. "And if Miss Ferreira should happen to get careless or nervous with the trigger, your death would not be on my conscience. Come on, Tom, let's get going. You start the engine."

So saying, he departed for the pilot-house, and soon the *Miami* was chugging back toward shore, where Cicero, Murphy, Captain Ferreira and Charley Loy were taken on board. George and Scutari were promptly lifted from the deck and put to bed. Scarface relieved Terry of the pistol with which she had been guarding Nick. Arty had been located in the galley and untied. Then all hands, except the four drunks, were assembled in the mess-room.

Captain Ferreira warmly embraced his daughter, and then his eyes ranged over those present.

"Where's Si Greene?" he asked. "Did that dolphin get him?"

Scarface Jimmy's face sobered, and his eyes narrowed.

"Si has given up his life for this girl here," he reported. "Two sea-beasts—and they weren't mere dolphins either—pulled him under and fought over him, just as we reached the ship. We waited around, but the poor fellow never came to the top again."

"Moby Dick!" exclaimed the ship captain, horrified.

Terry's eyes flashed around at Nick Fratelli.

"It's all your fault!" she sobbed. "Mr. Greene was a good, good man."

So saying, she jumped at him, but several of the men seized her and held her away.

"Nick has been guilty of mutiny on the high seas," announced Captain Ferreira. "The very least penalty is to be kept in irons until the end of the trip."

"I'll gladly supply the irons," cut in Mike Murphy, the ex-policeman, fishing his pair of handcuffs out of his pocket, and handing them over to his chief.

Still glowering, the burly Italian was untied and then man-acled.

"I'll give you this much freedom for the present," announced Scarface, "until I decide whether to keep you in irons for the rest of the trip, as Ferreira suggests, or to turn you loose alto-gether."

Then the party broke up for a few moments' rest, while Charley Loy prepared grub. Arty made a bee-line to his beloved radio; and, to the surprise of every one, got a station almost immediately.

Some one appeared to be broadcasting a speech. But it was in some utterly strange and outlandish language. Furthermore, the dial-setting did not correspond to any station on the earth's surface, most of which were marked in the little radio fan's log.

CHAPTER V

THE SECOND INVASION

"LITTLE ARTY'S GOT Sydney, Australia, at last," Cicero Tony snickered, as the ex-jockey adjusted the radio with loving care.

"Sydney, me eye," scornfully retorted Arty. "They don't speak Choctaw in Australia. This must be one of the broadcasting stations of the underworld. Probably a bedtime story."

"Do they speak Choctaw in hell?" Schultz snapped back.

"They don't have bedtime, anyhow," put in Mike Murphy. "It's always noon down here."

"There aren't any broadcasting stations in this country," asserted Tom Jones. "That is, unless Redmond and Selkirk, those two aviators that preceded us here, have developed them since last fall. I think that Arty has got some regular outside-world station, probably in Russia, from the way the language sounds."

Charley Loy, with food, cut off further debate. Also Arty, in attempting to improve the receptivity, lost the wave-length and was unable to get it again. Perhaps the station had stopped sending.

After supper they all turned in, the *Miami* having been moored to the shore.

At breakfast the four drunken mutineers appeared, George, Scutari, the Swede, and the Eskimo Friday. They all had bad headaches and were feeling pretty rocky, so they ate nothing, and merely drank some black coffee.

Immediately following the meal Little Arty tuned in the radio again, and instantly got the same station as before.

Several groaned with disgust; but Swede, sick as he was, pricked up his ears with interest.

"Wassamatter, Swede?" asked the Syrian. "Is that stuff language?"

"Yah!" replied Johnson eagerly.

"Where from, do you think?"

"Sveden, I gass. Or Norvay. Or Danmark."

Scarface now snapped to attention.

"What are they saying?" he asked. "Can you make out?"

"Yah!" replied Johnson, still listening intently. "They say one man fly scooter—"

"Glider?"

"Yah, glider. He say he fly scooter up nort' and see strange boat two hun'ert and fifty mile nort'east of plateau city. So t'ey better send up Vikings in many boats to see if ve mean funny business."

Scarface Jimmy leaped to his feet with his black eyes flashing.

"We've got our bearings," he shouted. "That thing we thought was a pterodactyl was really one of their scout-planes. We are two hundred and fifty miles northeast of our destination.

"So, Captain, set her course southwest, and let's go!"

"But which way *is* southwest?" asked Ferreira.

"You, a ship-captain!" began Scarface.

BUT THE Portuguese interrupted: "Do these inner-world Swede Vikings consider east to be on the *right* of north as it ought to be, or do they consider east to be on the left of *north*, as it really is down here?"

"Damfino," replied Scarface, stumped for once. "What do you think, Tom?"

"It seems to me," said the Harvard man slowly, "that when the expedition of Bishop Uppri was blown here in 1121, they couldn't possibly have known where they were. Even if they had known, they would have lacked the scientific training to figure out that 'east is west, and west is east' inside the earth—and their descendants would have kept the same direction-ideas. Accordingly, when this scout reported that we were northeast of their city, he meant northwest. Furthermore, as we went over the polar rim about a hundred and fifty miles west of the point where Eric and Angus did, this checks with that. So we ought to steer southeast."

"That's all very well," replied Ferreira. "First the boss says southwest, and then you say southeast. Which is right?"

"We're both right," asserted Tom Jones. "Steer four points to starboard of south."

"Let's go," added Scarface.

"Try an' do it," objected Captain Ferreira. "There's nothing but land in that direction."

"Can't we skirt the land?" asked Tom.

"Don't you remember," replied Ferreira, "how it looked from the top of that mountain we climbed? The land goes on forever."

"I have it," exclaimed Scarface. "Let's go back north, round the point of this land, and then strike southeast, or southwest, or whichever it is. Let's go!"

So that was the course they laid, skirting the shore to the northward around the cape, and then straight out to sea "four points to starboard south."

Two days—or, rather, two sleeps—later, land appeared ahead. Through the ship's telescope they could see a high rocky plain. And out of the middle of the plain rose a small and precipitous plateau, crowned with stone buildings.

"This is it, at last!" exclaimed Scarface Jimmy. "They know that we are here, so concealment now would be a waste of time. We must land at once, and attack before reënforcements arrive from their city to the south."

"I tank you make wan beeg mistake fight all t'ose Svede," remarked the Scandinavian member of the party half to himself.

The five men jumped as the tree crashed to the ground.

Captain Ferreira announced, "It will be four or five hours at least before we can reach the shore, though it's the devil of a job to judge distances on a sea that curves up, instead of down, and has no horizon."

"In that case," commanded Scarface, "everybody except Ferreira and Jones had better turn in and snatch some sleep, so that we shall all be fresh for whatever may be ahead of us. This eternal noonday sun has one advantage: we can pick our days and nights to suit our own convenience."

So every one, except the pilot and the engineer, went to bed.

A considerable time later Tom Jones entered the bunk room and roused them all from their slumbers.

"The *Miami* is about to dock," he announced with a grin. "Last call for dinner in the dining car."

The men "hit the deck" and started to dress. Cicero Tony Schultz, ordinarily very slovenly, made a wild dash to the galley for a cup of hot water, and started to shave.

Little Arty looked at him long and suspiciously, then announced with a snicker, "Hey, gang, laugh this off—our Cicero is sheiking himself up, to make a hit with all the beautiful corn-fed Swede girls when we land."

"He is, at that!" snorted Nick Fratelli. "Guess he figures there'll be a welcome for a Dutch boy-friend, with a bunch of blond what-do-you-call-'em—Nordics—around."

Cicero growled, inarticulate with angry embarrassment.

THERESA did not join them at the early meal, nor was there any sound of movement in her cabin, Scarface warned the men to make no noise near the cabin. "If she doesn't wake up, so much the better. I don't want to take her ashore, and I never did like to argue with a woman."

All through breakfast, Swede Johnson was muttering to himself. Finally some one demanded to know what was biting him.

"T'ose Viking von't be so easy, I tank not," he grumbled. "I tank you make von great mistake."

Nick looked at him shrewdly, and took occasion to lean over and murmur a few words to him as Scarface left the table to go on deck.

When they finally assembled outside the mess-room, they looked out on a crescent-shaped beach, backed by abrupt cliffs which were crested by forest. There was no break in the cliffs as far as eye could reach, but while they were steep, they were broken up and looked as if they might be safe to climb with care.

"Not wishing to get bitten twice in the same spot," announced Scarface Jimmy, "I shall leave Nick Fratelli behind, still in irons, and in the custody of Mike Murphy. All the rest of you men will come with me, except of course the Chink. Thus I shan't be taking any chances on another drunken orgy. I shall rather need this ship, you know, for further operations."

Each of the nine members of the shore-party was furnished a rifle, an automatic, plenty of ammunition, and several days' supply of compressed rations.

Murphy rowed them ashore in the tender.

Scarface, in his commodore's uniform, lined up his squad of eight sailors on the beach, and had them present arms to Mike Murphy, as Charley Loy leaned nonchalantly over the rail above them with a broad grin on his face. It seemed a bit too much dog. But, at that, the nine on the beach did present a very military—or rather naval—appearance, in their smart sailor uniforms, with rifles, ammunition belts, pistols in holsters, and packs. Scarface Boston Jimmy always had a good eye for the picturesque.

The ceremony over, the "commodore" led the way up the face of the cliff, closely followed by Tom, Arty, and Ferreira. It was a difficult climb, and they did not notice that the other five were lagging behind. Aboard the *Miami*, Charley Loy had already disappeared into the galley.

"Murphy," softly called Syrian George, dropping on his knees on the beach and appearing to examine something in the sand, "you're a good Irishman. Come here and tell me if this ain't a shamrock."

Murphy stepped out of the beached rowboat and strode across the sand to the little group. Swede Johnson stepped behind him and crashed his pistol-butt against the base of the Irishman's skull, and Murphy sagged, to be soundlessly eased to the ground by Scutari. Murphy was out cold, perhaps dead.

"So much for cops," muttered George. "How about pottin' those guys up on the cliff?"

"No use," Cicero decided. "We'll just leave 'em here for the Vikings to play wit'. Come on, gang."

At a run the five—Cicero, Scutari, George, Swede Johnson, and the Eskimo—made their way to the boat and shoved off. A very few strokes and they were at the *Miami*, clambering aboard.

It had all been done so quietly that the first warning to reach the panting cliff-climbers was the sound of the *Miami's* engines. They clung precariously to the steep incline as they craned around, and realized how they had again been tricked. Scarface showed his qualities of leadership by his instant decision.

"Quick! Make it to the top of the cliff!"

Back on the *Miami*, Nick the Rat appeared on deck, still handcuffed. George the Syrian, who had frisked Mike for his keys, announced as much, and dug into his pocket for them.

"Why didn't you plug those four birds?" demanded Nick viciously. The men looked at him like kicked dogs who had expected to be patted. Then they stared accusingly at Cicero, He hastened to explain:

"We was makin' a clean get-away. Why start a gun battle and run the risk of gettin' plugged?"

"Fool!" Fratelli sneered. "Hurry up and get them, now, while they're still on the cliff."

AT THE command, some of the men unslung their rifles and blazed away at the cliff-side. Chunks of rock flew as the exposed four scrambled wildly up toward safety, Captain Ferreira suddenly let go his hold, and seemed to float backward, then tumbled swiftly head over heels down to the beach below.

Tom Jones was first to reach the brink of the cliff, and scuttled behind a bowlder. Then, unslinging his rifle, he poured a hot fire on the *Miami's* sharpshooters. It was well for Little Arty and Scarface that he did so, for the Swede's rifle was knocked out of his hands, and the others on the boat dodged for shelter. Under cover of Tom's fire, the two on the cliff-side reached safety.

Scarface's first shot, intended for Fratelli, hit George the Syrian instead, as that unlucky mutineer reached over to unlock Nick's handcuffs. George staggered at the impact, tottered wildly, and then tumbled over the *Miami's* rail into the sea. But the keys jangled to the deck, and Fratelli awkwardly scooped them up with both tethered hands. Then, as more shots whistled perilously near him, he dashed through one of the doorways of the boat, and was lost to view.

The marooned trio blazed away vengefully, and their bullets repeatedly splintered the windows of the pilot-house; but, as none of the enemy happened to be in there, this didn't do much good—or harm, depending on the point of view.

The *Miami* backed straight out. Finally it became evident that some one aboard had at last taken charge of the wheel, for her straight backing changed to a gentle curve until she lay broadside of them. Then her engines were reversed, she started ahead, and curved forward out to sea. No further shots were fired from on board.

"They're saving their powder, Arty," said Scarface, getting to his feet. "So we'd better save ours, too. Are you all right, Tom?"

"Yes; but where's Ferreira?"

The *Miami* was nearly out of range now, so they crept to the edge of the cliff and looked down—to see two still, crumpled figures.

Leaving Scarface and Arty to cover him from possible attack from the *Miami*, Tom clambered back down the cliff. He found that Ferreira was beyond human aid, sprawled horribly at the cliff's foot with a broken neck.

But Murphy was only stunned. Hatfuls of water thrown in his face finally revived him, and in time he found that his dizziness was sufficiently abated so that he could attempt the climb, to join Scarface and Arty.

"Well, it's one heat for each," said the little jockey, Arty. "They got Ferreira, and we got George."

"Yeah?" drawled Scarface. "But Nick's ahead—for the time. He got the boat."

"And Theresa!" cried Tom.

CHAPTER VI

OUT OF THE FRYING PAN

ABOARD THE *MIAMI*, Nick Fratelli dashed through the door of the mess-room. Cicero Tony Schultz was inside, lying low.

"Afraid to get shot, eh?" sneered Nick. "Well, you just take these keys and let me loose, quick, or you'll be in worse danger than you'd be in on deck!"

But it required some time before the fumbling fingers of the German found the right key and slipped the handcuffs off the hands of his new leader.

Just as this was accomplished, Theresa, awakened by the shooting, came dewy-eyed and sleepy out of the doorway of her private stateroom, only to be immediately seized and manacled, before she had time to realize what a revolution had taken place.

This accomplished, Fratelli rushed to the pilot-house, and, crawling along the floor to avoid the bullets which were crashing through the windows, took hold of the wheel and brought the vessel around. Then, signaling full speed ahead to Scutari, who was in the engine room, Nick steered for open sea.

Swede Johnson had been shot only through the left hand, and had long since crawled to safety, followed by the Eskimo. Charley Loy had remained discreetly under his bunk during the entire disturbance.

When safely out of range from the shore, the *Miami* turned south, and finally tied up behind a small island, which looked as though it would make a good headquarters. Then the new leader of the gang gathered his forces in the mess-room.

There was Nick the Rat, himself. Charley Loy and Theresa, both sullen and reticent. Swede, with his left hand bandaged. Cicero, Scutari and Friday. And the black cat, misnamed Tabby.

The habitually sullen Italian gangster was almost genial.

"Boys," he began.

Theresa pouted.

"Ladies and gentlemen," he began again.

Theresa grinned.

Nick tried a third peroration. "Whereas in the course of—er—"

Theresa snickered. "Who d' you think you are—Captain Jimmy?"

"Look here, you little Portuguese guttersnipe," he growled, "if you don't stop handing me the raspberries, you get your face slapped, and besides, I'm going to—"

"Gee now, Mr. Fratelli," interrupted Terry beguilingly, "a nice kind gentleman like you wouldn't do that to poor little me, I'm sure."

Nick, quickly placated, smirked at her, and continued: "What I started to say was that we are now shut of that conceited fake navy-officer, and have a real man as leader, we're all set. I'm going to keep the booze locked up, just as he did."

Frowns all around.

"But I'm going to be much more liberal in handing it out."

Smiles again.

"Friday, here, has been teaching me to talk Eskimo language. Swede has been right, all along, in saying that it is foolish for a small party of us to try to buck all the Vikings. But, with Friday as interpreter, we can line up all the natives and use them to fight the Vikings with. I've got more brains than Jimmy, even if I don't read as many books, or talk as high-end as he does."

It was a long speech for the usually sullen Italian. Loud applause greeted the announcement.

Then Fratelli continued: "Now let's search the ship. But lay off the rum-lockers."

THE SEARCH disclosed the store of rifles and ammunition, beyond their wildest dreams. The two machine guns were promptly brought out and mounted in the bow and stern.

Then, while the Chink prepared a meal, assisted by Terry as well as was possible in her shackled condition, the others went ashore to explore the island. It turned out to be unusually devoid of underbrush, but thickly wooded, giving it a park-like appearance. In the ground, among the trees, were numerous large holes, each with a pile of earth in front of it.

"I tank von big boog," said Swede, looking cautiously down one of the holes.

"It must be a big bug, to make a hole like that!" replied Fratelli.

Just at that instant a pungent smell was wafted down the breeze, and Cicero, who had been some distance beyond them, came running back yelling: "Skunks! And *Gott in Himmel*, such skunks!"

And after him trotted two black-and-white striped animals about the size of bears. The entire party promptly clambered up the nearest tree, Swede nearly getting captured because hampered by his sore hand.

Luckily it turned out that the skunks couldn't climb, but they nosed about at the foot of the tree interminably—and odorously. The sun hung motionless in the center of the sky, and the two beasts seemed oblivious of the passage of time.

At last, however, they hurried away.

The five men were just about to descend, when Swede remarked: "I tank dey vere frighten' by somet'ing."

Quite true, for at that moment a long-haired, clumsy animal, considerably larger than an elephant, lumbered into sight. Its hind feet were placed squarely on the ground in walking like those of a bear or of a man, but the claws on its front feet were so long that it had to plant the sides of those feet, rather than the soles of them, on the ground. This gave it a curious, waddling gait.

Upon reaching the foot of their tree, this huge beast reared up on its hind legs and embraced the trunk with its fore legs.

"We're goners!" cried Cicero Tony. "*This* one can climb."

But, instead of climbing, it hooked its claws around the trunk and leaned backward. The tree swayed with the movement, nearly shaking off the men like five pieces of ripe fruit.

Holding on with one paw, the megatherium reached higher up with the other and took a new hold. The tree bent a little further. The process was repeated, and the tree bent still further.

The men, now almost within reach, scrambled higher among the branches. But the beast persisted in its slow inexorable tactics, and the tree bent lower and lower.

At last the men reached the top of the tree, and the top of the tree had been bent down so that it nearly touched the ground.

There seemed to be but one thing to do. The five men jumped, and ran for their lives to the shore.

But the beast did not pursue them. In fact, he seemed as oblivious of their presence as if they had been so many bugs. He sat on his haunches, calmly nibbling the tender shoots of the crown of the tree. It was for these, rather than for the men, that he had gone to all the trouble of hauling the tree to the ground.

BUT ONE misfortune followed another. As they reached the beach, they heard the chugging of a motor. The *Miami* was backing out into the sea, and already was clearly out of reach.

"Turn about is fair play," philosophically remarked Scutari.

"The hell you say!" roared Fratelli. "We left the others on the mainland with several days' rations, and within a few hours' walk of a civilized city. They wanted to go conquering the blamed thing, anyway. But here we are on a dinky little island, full of tree-pullers and over-sized skunks."

At that moment, the sound of the motors ceased.

"Quick," shouted Nick. "Who can swim?"

"I can, a little," replied Scutari.

"Then hop to it," commanded Nick. "Fetch me that boat."

Without waiting to strip, the Greek plunged in.

Meanwhile, on board the *Miami*, little Terry was holding the wheel in her manacled hands, and the Chinaman in the engine room was frantically trying to restart the stalled engine. The girl rang the bell several times for full speed ahead, and then rushed aft to see what was the matter.

She had scarcely entered the engine room when she heard a step on the deck, and knew it was one of Nick's men. Instantly she grappled with the startled Chinaman. So, when Scutari entered, dripping, it appeared as though a fight were in progress for the control of the boat.

"Gee, Mr. Scutari," she exclaimed, with pretended relief, as Scutari's pistol-threat halted the struggle, "Charley Loy started the engines and tried to make his get-away, but I stopped the engines. He couldn't be here and in the pilot-house both at once. Gee, Mr. Scutari, I'm glad you got here just in time."

"Charley," commanded the Greek, "you stay right here. Terry, you go to the wheel and steer her in shore again. You're a good kid. I'll see that Nick remembers you for this."

Charley Loy stared with bewilderment at Terry's retreating figure, but he said nothing. Saying nothing at the appropriate time is the chief accomplishment of the heathen Chinee.

Scutari had but little difficulty in starting the engine. The trouble was merely a disconnected wire, which he naturally assumed to have been Terry's work. So this lent plausibility to her story, which he never thought to question, anyway.

As the *Miami* neared the beach and stopped, Nick the Rat waded aboard and rushed into the pilot-house.

"You dirty little gutter-brat—" he began.

But Scutari, anticipating some such development, arrived just in time from the engine room and cut in with: "Chief, you've got her all wrong. It's her that saved the boat for us. The Chink tried to slip away, but she pulled one of the wires loose and stopped the engine. The two of them was fighting to get at the wire, when I came aboard."

"Is that so?" asked Nick, a bit incredulously.

"Gee, Mr. Fratelli, you didn't think I'd leave *you,* didja?" replied Terry archly, and Nick the Rat was vain enough to believe her.

"Let's get away from this damn' island," urged Cicero, glancing furtively back at the woods.

"Let's feed the Chink to the skunks first," suggested Scutari.

"Let's not!" emphatically replied Nick. "It's more important for us to eat, than for the skunks to."

"And I tell you," hastily added Theresa, "you take these awful things off my wrists, and I'll cook you up a beautiful cake for supper, or whatever time of day it is."

She smiled her sweetest on the already smitten gangster, who promptly removed the handcuffs.

"That's a fine idea of yours about the cake," said he, smirking, "but you just wait here a moment, my little cutie, until I go into the galley and give that dirty Chink a piece of my mind. I'll put the fear of God into him, so he'll never dare try to double-cross *me* again."

And he swaggered aft to berate the cook.

AS THE *Miami* once more put to sea, with Fratelli at the wheel, the Greek at the engine and Charley and Theresa in the galley, the three others repaired to the bunk room.

"This is something like!" remarked Cicero to Swede and Friday. "Why, before, with that crowd on board, there wasn't room enough to swing a cat by the tail."

"Vy you vant to sving a cat by tail?" asked Swede.

"Just a little hobby of mine," replied Cicero. Then, half to himself: "Why not! That black Tabby cat had been our Jonah. Here goes. Come on, if you want to see some fun."

So saying, he rushed out on deck, followed by the other two. Tabby was peacefully sunning himself.

A moment later Theresa heard a frantic miaou; and, glancing out one of the galley portholes, saw her precious kitty, held by the end of its tail in one of Cicero's large hands, as he whirled the yowling feline round and round his head.

With a scream, the girl rushed on deck, but she was too late. As she flung herself upon Cicero Tony, he let go the tail, and the black cat, with a howl like the drone of a 75 mm. projectile, described a perfect parabola in the air and hit the water with a smack.

Swede, who had been in France in 1918, watched the spot for a moment and then remarked:

"A dud."

A second splash occurred where the cat had fallen. Some denizen of the deep had risen to the bait.

"Delayed fuse," murmured Swede.

"Oh, you beast, you beast," cried Theresa, pounding and clawing Cicero with her little fists, but Swede pulled her away and shook her, and sent her back to the galley in tears.

Then the three men returned to the bunk room, Swede remarking: "I tank it bad luck kill a cat."

"Worse luck to have a damn' black cat aboard," growled Cicero.

Shortly thereafter Nick called Swede to take the wheel. Then he himself entered the galley.

Smirking at Terry, he said: "Well, my little sweetheart, how's the cake coming?"

"Gee, Mr. Fratelli," said the girl, with tears in her eyes, "won't you do something to that awful Dutchman? He threw Tabby overboard and a fish ate him."

"Ate who? Tony?"

"No. Tabby," replied Terry, smiling through her tears. "You're a big strong man, Mr. Fratelli. Won't you put Tony in irons or something, just to please me?"

"I'd do anything to please you, girlie," asserted Nick, "but you've got to be nice to me."

"Gee, Mr. Fratelli, but you're great!"

"Call me Nick."

"Gee, Nick, but you're great!"

He held out one hand tentatively toward her, but she edged shyly away, saying: "I've gotter finish the cake now. See you after supper."

So, with that promise in his ears, Fratelli went to the bunk room for a conference with Friday, the Eskimo.

THE CAKE was a great success. All enjoyed the meal except Cicero, who, being in irons for the delectation of the queen and the gratification of Nick's pride of power, could hardly be expected to be very jovial. Terry particularly made up to the chief, who smirked and smiled and behaved quite unlike his usual morose self.

After the meal, as the girl started to enter her room, Nick remarked pointedly, with a wave of his hand toward the door: "The captain's cabin will be occupied by the new captain, from now on."

Terry was a bit taken aback for a moment, then smiled her sweetest on him and said: "I've got to help Charley with the dishes for a few moments. Wait for me in your cabin."

Then she and the Chinaman started clearing away the table. During the meal the boat had been permitted just to drift. Now Fratelli ordered Swede to man the wheel and Scutari to start up the engine again. The Eskimo, he directed to take Cicero to the bunk room. He himself began moving his belongings into his new quarters. He could scarcely wait for the dishwashing to be over.

As the last load of dishes were being carried to the galley, Charley Loy said quietly to his helper: "Velly bad. Velly bad. Makee tlubble for little girl."

"Oh, I'm all right," asserted Terry, with a toss of her head, "I asked that bum Fratelli to wait for me; and, believe me, he'll wait!"

The *Miami* was now skirting the shore of the mainland.

"Good-by, Charley," continued the girl. "You're a good scout, so I'll give you a bit of advice. When Nick gets tired of waiting, and asks you where I am, it would be wise for you to tell him that I went to his cabin. Savvy?"

The Oriental beamed on her.

"You velly blight girl," said he.

Meanwhile Nick Fratelli, at peace with the world, and very proud of himself as a gang leader and ladies' man, waited in his newly-acquired cabin. He waited with keen anticipation.

Then he waited with impatience. Then he waited with growing anger, and finally with suspicion.

At last he strode back to the galley. The dishwashing was completed. Charley Loy was industriously sweeping.

"Where's Terry?" roared Fratelli.

The Chinaman jumped, as though startled. Then turning his artless poker-face toward Nick, he said: "Little girl just left minute before. Say she go see her boy fliend now. Solly. Velly solly."

And he resumed his sweeping.

"Search the ship," bellowed Fratelli, rushing out of the kitchen.

Quickly he roused the rest of the crew. The ship was stopped, and all joined in the search. But at last it became quite evident that Miss Theresa Ferreira was no longer on board.

"Chief," whined Cicero, "you done me dirt. You put me in irons just to please that moll. I'm loyal to you. Won't you take them things off'n me?"

"Tony," replied Fratelli apologetically, "forgive me. But if I ever get my hands on that dirty little Portuguese guttersnipe again, she'll pay for this! That's all I have to say."

"Well, chief," said Cicero vengefully, "it's a cinch you never will see her again, for by now she's et up by fishes, just like that cat was."

And he smiled reminiscently.

Nick looked sad.

"Poor little kid."

AT THAT moment, many miles to the north of them, a pathetic feminine figure, clad in a wet and clinging male sailor suit, was bravely trudging northward along the beach. As she wearily stumbled through the sand, she was glad to be safe from Fratelli, but she was tired and thirsty, and utterly devoid of any plans.

Finally she sat down on a rock to rest, and as she gazed listlessly around her, her interest was aroused by a large black and white object, which the waves were carrying in toward shore. It seemed to be a black fish about ten feet long with a white belly, floating belly-up. But there was one unnatural feature about it, namely, a small round fuzzy black rosette, wiggling violently in the middle of the white expanse.

Momentarily forgetting her fatigue, the girl jumped up and ran down to the water's edge, where the dead "fish" was already bumping upon the pebbles. It was a porpoise-like reptile, an ichthyosaurus.

"Miaou," said the dead fish.

Theresa started backward in surprise, and at that moment the fuzzy object, protruding from the center of the fish's belly, gave a lurch, the white skin of the reptilian fish split the rest of the way, and Tabby followed its head out of the opening, stretching itself and arching its back.

"You darling kitty," exclaimed Terry, snatching it up and hugging it to her bosom, in spite of its slimy condition. "I thought you were gone forever! That mean old Cicero called

you his Jonah, so you picked out a pocket-edition whale for
yourself and got saved! It's a good joke on him."

She felt better instantly. Here was a companion for her. A
few minutes later she lay stretched on the beach in the warm
sun, while Tabby lay beside her, purring and lapping himself,
and the dead ichthyosaurus bumped up and down forgotten
on the pebbles.

When the cat at last considered himself presentable again,
he arose languidly, stretched first his back and then one hind
leg after the other, looked up at the girl and purred, and then
trotted off into the woods which lined the beach. Theresa got
up and followed.

Tabby led her promptly to a small spring, where they both
drank copiously. Then, without a word of warning, the cat
slipped quietly into the underbrush and disappeared.

A wave of loneliness suddenly engulfed the brave little girl.
Slumping down beside the spring, she burst into tears. But after
a while she dried her eyes. Perhaps Tabby would come back
again.

He did. He returned dragging with him a funny dead animal
as large as himself, which he laid proudly at his mistress's feet.
Then he rubbed against her, purring loudly and ostentatiously.

The dead animal looked like an overgrown guinea pig, with
long legs and a mule-like head and tail.

"Oh, Tabby dear," said the girl, "I can't eat raw bunny. Here,
you take it, while I hunt for some berries."

The cat looked at her and at the rejected gift sadly and then
started a repast on the carcass.

Theresa found a few small berries, but their taste was acrid
and she mistrusted them. At last she came to a tree which bore
orange-like fruit as large as pumpkins. She poked one off the
tree with a pole, but was unable to lift it.

The skin smelled unmistakably like an orange, so she dug
into the skin, and found it to be several inches thick. But the

fruit skinned readily, and as readily divided into segments. In fact, it was exactly like an orange inside.

Peeling the thin transparent membrane off one of the segments, Theresa was soon regaling herself with the cells of luscious orange-colored and orange-flavored liquid which made up the interior of the segment, and which she plucked out and ate one by one.

Their meal over, she lay down, with Tabby snuggled close beside her, and soon was fast asleep.

But her sleep was not untroubled. Presently she dreamed that she was in a close and stuffy room. She opened her eyes to awake.

A fetid breath was blowing in her face. She looked up into the slavering jaws of a gigantic dog-like head!

CHAPTER VII

THE RED MAMMOTH

MEANWHILE Scarface Boston Jimmy, with Tom Jones, late of Harvard, and Arty, the little old jockey, had sadly buried the body of Antone Pease Ferreira. Mike Murphy's head still ached frightfully from the pistol-butt blow, but otherwise he seemed in fit shape.

There was no point in staying where they were, and no place to go, except toward the Viking city. So the four set off together up a trail which they found leading inland from the top of the cliff. After several hours of hiking, and stopping once for lunch, their road finally led to the edge of a level plain, across which, a half mile or so away, they could see the steep cliffs of the plateau which they had observed from the sea.

Persons were gathered in one spot on the edge of the cliff, and even as the watchers gazed up from within the cover of the wood, those persons disappeared one by one, only to reappear among the bushes at the foot of the cliff. A glider slid off the crest of the plateau, circled the plain, and returned to its starting point.

"Just the way it was in that *Argosy* story," Scarface exulted. "We're here at last!"

"Yeah?" replied Little Arty pessimistically. "And what good does it do you? Are you planning for the four of us to attack all those squareheads?"

"Not exactly," said Jimmy. "We must use strategy now."

"Why not use just plain human decency?" suggested Tom Jones. "Come to the Vikings as friends, and mean it. Eric and Angus played square—"

"Played squarehead, you mean," interrupted Arty.

"Well, anyway," continued Jones, "it worked, didn't it? Eric and Angus are now sitting on top of the world—or inside the world—oh, it's all so complicated! Anyway, let's try the same tactics."

"We may be forced to that, as a last resort," admitted Scarface.

"Say, what about Theresa?" Tom asked suddenly. "Here we've been worrying about dreams of empire, and lamenting because Nick Fratelli has walked off with our boat, when all the while that poor little girl is in the clutches of those roughnecks. Mr. Lefavour, sir, we've just got to side in with the Vikings, and get them to help us rescue Theresa."

Scarface looked at Tom appraisingly.

"I had thought of that myself." He was obviously torn between two ruling passions. "I shall settle that question. Come on."

So together the four set forth across the plain toward the spot where they had seen the Vikings emerge.

They had little difficulty in finding the hole in the bushes. Crawling through it, they came to a crack extending vertically upward in the face of the cliff, and up this crack they clambered, by virtue of many footholds, handholds and kneeholds in its sides. But when they reached the top, the way was barred by a stone slab set firmly across the opening. Try as they would, they could not budge it. They shouted repeatedly, but no answer came. No one heeded them.

So, at last, they climbed down again, and crawled out through the bushes at the base.

After staring disconsolately for a while at the heights, they withdrew to the shelter of the woods, where they had supper and then slept, taking turns watching one by one, so that they would know if the expedition from the plateau returned, or if any further signs of life showed at the brink of the cliff. But there were no developments.

FINALLY Scarface roused them. "I've had enough of sitting here like this, doing nothing. We ought to be getting busy rescuing that girl. This isn't proving anything."

"Let's walk around the foot of the plateau," suggested Tom. "Perhaps we can attract some attention somewhere. If not, we shall just have to come back and wait here, until that expedition returns. I wish they'd hurry. Every minute may count with poor little Terry."

So they started circling the base of the cliff, munching their breakfast as they walked, and shouting and hallooing from time to time.

And at last an answer came to one of their calls. But not from the cliff-top. Instead, it came from around a bend ahead of them. And it was a most peculiar sound, more like a squeaky Fourth of July tin horn than anything else—a giant's horn, loud as a calliope.

"Queer bugles these Swedes have," remarked Murphy.

"Bugle, hell! Look what broke loose from the circus!" yelled Little Arty, who was in the lead.

Around the bend, at a ponderous canter, came an enormous elephant-like creature with long red fur, trumpeting loudly as he came—a mammoth!

"Run!" cried Tom, and the four of them scattered in as many directions, as the beast bore down upon them.

Three of them were sure of escape, for the woolly red elephant could not chase all four at once. The mammoth selected Scarface Jimmy as his victim. Clumsy though the huge animal appeared to be, he could run as fast as a man, or a little faster. So Scarface shed his dignity without a thought and fled as never before in his life.

Straight toward a clump of trees he ran, and seized a branch and pulled himself up, just in time. It was not enough merely to gain the low-hanging branch. Up the tree he scrambled, scraping off bark and clothing and skin. He had scarce got above the level of the beast's head before it crashed against the trunk with an impact which nearly hurled the man from his perch.

Then, backing up, the mammoth reared and reached for the man with its trunk. Scarface, scrambling upward again, just barely eluded the snake-like menace. Thereupon the mammoth withdrew for a short distance and began a series of battering-ram rushes at the tree.

Scarface hung on for dear life each time, and thus escaped being shaken off; but the tree itself gradually yielded at the roots, and began to bend more and more, under the successive blows.

The elephant, finding that the tree had begun to loosen at the roots, changed his tactics and, placing his huge head square-ly against the trunk, braced all four of his legs and began to push steadily. Inch by inch, the tree gave; there was nothing Scarface could do but climb higher and higher.

CHAPTER VIII

THE VIKINGS

TERRY STARED UP at those slavering jaws. For a long, ghastly moment she lay motionless with terror, tensing as one does when trying to wake from an unbearable nightmare. Then something slapped against her side.

It was the lashing tail of Tabby, suddenly awakened, and confronted with the largest dog that the poor cat had ever seen in all its nine lives.

Now, when a dog chases a cat, the cat flees.

But when a dog corners a cat, the cat goes absolutely berserk and attacks after the general manner of a rapidly rotating buzz saw.

Tabby, suddenly awakened, imagined himself cornered by the huge hyænodont, and so sprang full in the beast's face, with every hair on end, and four sets of claws rotating at full speed.

The last that Theresa saw of the two animals, the hyænodont, with its tail between its legs, and emitting loud but very dog-like yelps, was galloping off for dear life through the woods, with Tabby perched on the beast's back, feet close together, claws digging in, back arched, and inflated tail erect.

Partly through sheer nervous relief, and partly because of the real humor of the situation, Theresa sat up and laughed uncontrollably. Finally she arose, drank and washed at the spring, and ate from another of the huge orange-fruit.

Just as she was finishing her breakfast, she heard voices approaching through the woods. Hastily backing behind some bushes, she lay in their protecting concealment.

In that direction, which was uphill from where she lay, there was a high rocky ledge. As she gazed, a bronze helmet appeared, surmounted with a pair of golden wings. Beneath the helmet, she saw long yellow hair, a rugged, tanned face, blue eyes, and a wavy yellow mustache. A scarlet cape, flung across massive shoulders, was caught at the throat with a gold buckle.

The man's sinewy arms bore bracelets of various metals.

His left hand clasped the wooden shaft of a steel-tipped spear. A shirt of chain-mail hung almost to his knees. A sword-belt, slung across the hips, supported a cross-hilted slender blade. He had long leggings, strapped with crisscrossed leather thongs.

The first Viking was followed by another, somewhat similarly garbed, except that the second wore a yellow cape and a purple shirt, and carried a spiked club and a burnished shield.

After him came an older man, with flowing white beard, and a green cape and scarlet shirt.

Others followed, some with clubs and shields, and some with spears and shields, until about twenty warriors stood on the summit of the rock.

"Gee, ain't they swell!" breathed Terry to herself, lost in admiration for these supermen out of the past. And then, remembering that these were the enemy, the people from whom her expedition intended to wrest the dominion of this continent, a sudden terror swept over her.

Losing all discretion in her fright, she jumped to her feet and fled precipitately, frantically, through the wood.

"*Staap!*" bellowed several lusty voices behind her. It sounded like English, and there was no question as to its meaning. Perhaps, she thought, it really was English. Perhaps these fantastically clothed men were not Vikings after all, but Americans. Perhaps they were only movie actors.

Most illiterates and most young folks have an absolute mental gap on the subject of location and distance. Although they can uncannily find their way around, yet it would not surprise them in the least to discover San Francisco lying a few hours east of New York, or to walk from Boston to London, England, in the course of an afternoon, without crossing any water.

Theresa was both young and illiterate, and so it is not strange that she harbored the idea of meeting a motion picture troupe in the center of the earth.

SHE TURNED the possibility over in her mind as she ran on, and was just about to give up anyway when a heavy hand fell on her shoulder and put a stop to her flight.

The hand wheeled her roughly around, and another hand grasped her other shoulder. She looked up, affrighted, into a pair of kind and rather puzzled blue eyes beneath a winged helmet. She was in the grip of the Viking leader, the one of the red cloak and the chain-mail. But he did not seem so formidable, close up. And his intentions appeared to be friendly.

"Gee, but you had me frightened for a moment, sir," said Terry, with her most engaging smile.

In reply, she was deluged with questions in a strange tongue, at which she was able only to shake her head in bewilderment. The chief remarked something significantly to one of his followers.

"Say, do you belong to Eric Redmond?" asked Terry.

"Yah, yah, Eric Redmond," replied the chief and again remarked something significantly to his follower.

After further conversation among the Vikings, the chief turned back to Terry and said, *"Komm!"*

So she came. The party set off briskly into the interior, the girl in her blue and white sailor suit walking proudly by the side of the Viking chief, a strange conjunction of nautical styles, eight hundred years apart.

But the girl soon tired. The young Viking took her by the arm and helped her along. She didn't mind this in the least.

Finally her escort had to call on one of his men to help him, and from then on the two practically carried the poor girl between them.

Hours dragged after hours. The men began grumbling about being hungry, and about the delay. When at last they reached an encampment, Theresa was sound asleep standing up; and the moment they halted she slid to the ground completely oblivious.

The Vikings then cooked and ate and slept, and when Theresa came to her senses she was lying in a skin tent on a pile of furs. Outdoors, her companions—or captors—were busily preparing their morning meal.

The poor child was famished. Her feet hurt her terribly. But, apart from that, she was fresh and rested.

"Hullo, folks," said she, coming to the door of her tent. "Gee, but that breakfast smells good."

"Hullo," they replied with a strange intonation to the word. Then there followed other words, which she was completely at a loss to understand.

"I don't know what you're saying," said she with an engaging smile, "but I accept your kind invitation."

Whereupon she sat down and helped herself to some of the food. Instantly the grim warriors crowded around her, and literally fell over each other in their eagerness to be of service to her.

The most eager was the boy in chain-mail, with the yellow curls and drooping yellow mustache. His helmet was off now, and he appeared even younger, not over twenty, in spite of the mustache. Terry was in her element. And yet, if she had but considered, there was no reason to believe that these Vikings as yet suspected her sex.

TWO NIGHTS—if one can call them nights, with the central sun hanging ever in the zenith—had passed since the girl had

slipped over the side of the *Miami,* to escape from the clutches of Nick Fratelli and his accomplices.

The baffled gangster, in spite of his certainty that she had
been devoured by some sea monster, had run the ship back
along the shore in search of her; but, thanks to plenty of mis-
information from Charley Loy, Nick had so far misjudged the
time of her departure that he didn't run back anywhere near far
enough.

Finally the hunt had been abandoned, the *Miami* had been
tied to the shore, and, after another meal, the gang had all
turned in for a sleep.

After breakfast, the Rat called a council of war of his cohorts,
and announced his plans.

Said he: "I figure, from Eric Redmond's story, that there is
some sort of town of these here Skraelings—which is what the
savages are called—quite a distance south of the plateau city
of the Vikings. I want those Skraelings, and I want them pronto.
I have a damn' good idea that our old boss, Scarface, will team
up with the Vikings, now that he finds himself without many
men. We stand a good chance of getting run out of here if we
don't do something quick. Scarface isn't licked yet. Too bad all
you bums got lit up, the other time we skipped out on him, or
we wouldn't have him to worry about now."

"I tank you make wan beeg mistake call me a boom," replied
Swede Johnson. "You ain't ban Scarface Yimmy."

"No, I 'ain't ban Scarface Yimmy,'" retorted Fratelli; "and
what's more, if you cut loose another wisecrack like that, you
won't be Swede Yohnson any longer; do you get me?"

"Yah," admitted the Swede.

Nick then chained the Chinese to one of the deck-rings, by
means of the pair of handcuffs which had been Mike Murphy's
chief contribution to events aboard the *Miami.* Leaving food
and water within Charley's reach, Nick started inland with
Cicero, Swede, Scutari and Friday, all five fully armed and ra-
tioned.

The terrain at this point was an open, park-like field, through which they pressed rapidly at right angles to the coast; until after about an hour, they struck a well-marked trail running north and south.

"Are any of youse Boy Scouts?" inquired Nick. "Because if you are, here's your chance to figure out which way this sidewalk runs."

All examined it intently, but with no particular purpose in mind.

Then Swede announced: "I tank it run both vays."

"Of course it does, you dumb-bell," retorted Nick, exasperated.

"I tank you make wan beeg mistake call me doom-bell," said Swede calmly, but he wisely refrained from any comment about Nick's not being Scarface.

"I have it," exclaimed Cicero, "Let's toss for it. Heads we go north. Tails we go south."

He flipped a coin. Nick stooped and picked it up.

"Heads!" said he, putting the coin in his own pocket.

So they started north.

After a time they ate, then trudged on some more, then ate again.

"Time to sleep," announced their leader.

"Say, we forgot our blankets," objected Cicero.

"What do you think this is, anyway," sneered Nick, "a hotel? This is war!"

"Yeah?" asked Cicero. "Well, we had blankets in the last war I was in."

"You must have been in the Audience Department then," retorted Nick, "for there was lots of times in France when we infantry didn't have no blankets at all."

"Shut up!" exclaimed Scutari. "I hear some one coming."

American gangsters may not be woodsmen, but they can certainly take to cover like Indians the moment they sense danger.

Consequently the Viking band coming down the path saw nothing to arouse their suspicion.

CHAPTER IX

ON THE VIKING TRAIL

THERE WERE FIVE of the Vikings. As they came into sight along the path, Nick the Rat whispered to his gang, who lay, with rifles ready, concealed behind a clump of bushes: "When I say the word, give 'em the works."

"I tank—" began Swede.

"Fire!" shouted Nick, and out blazed five rifles.

Two Vikings fell. The three others stood irresolute for a moment. Then, hurling their spears before them, they rushed full at the bush. Once more the rifles blazed, and then the gangsters leaped to their feet and met drawn swords with the roar of automatics.

It was all over in an instant. The five Vikings lay on the ground, four of them motionless, the fifth propped up on one elbow, with his other hand to his chest, coughing.

Scutari had fallen flat on his back, with a spear through his heart. Nick Fratelli's right forearm was pinned to his side with a slender Viking sword which he was frantically trying to push out with his left hand. Cicero, torn and bleeding about one shoulder, had dropped his automatic, and was leaning against a tree, feeling of the injured part. Friday, the Eskimo, had fled.

Swede Johnson stood over the dying Viking. The latter coughed and murmured something. Swede bent low to catch the words, then straightened up.

"The curse of Thor!" he muttered in sudden superstitious horror.

The Viking coughed once more, transfixed Cicero with a baleful glance and dropped prone on the grass.

"I tank—" began Swede, but Nick interrupted him:

"Can the chatter, and pull out this butcher knife. Easy now," as Swede obliged him.

The hole in Nick's side turned out to be merely a flesh-wound, but the blade had penetrated his forearm right between the two bones.

As Swede dexterously tore off a part of Nick's shirt and bandaged the arm, the wounded man growled: "The nerve of those squareheads, fighting against all our guns."

"Dey vere Vikings!" asserted Swede proudly.

Friday reappeared, and was given quite a dressing-down by Fratelli in the Eskimo's guttural tongue. Then the four took Scutari's rifle, pistol, food and ammunition, and the helmets, swords, bucklers and other trappings of the dead enemy. Fratelli helped himself to a purple cloak which struck his fancy; Cicero took a jeweled dagger, marked with a jade swastika.

Laden with booty, the four started back down the trail, leaving the bodies of the five Vikings and Scutari, with perfect unconcern, to rot beneath the sweltering beams of the central sun.

"I tank—" began Swede.

"You think too much," interrupted Nick Fratelli testily. "What *I* think is that we better not get within reach of any more Vikings if we can help it. Come on, you guys, or we'll be in a jam."

ABOUT the time when Nick and his gang had started out on the exploring trip, Scarface and his party began their circuit of the plateau, which was to end in their utter rout by a woolly mammoth, which had run Scarface himself up a tree.

The beast had then continued to bunt at the tree, until the tree leaned at such an angle that the brute's head could no longer secure a purchase against the slanting bark.

"No, thanks, Mr. Jones, I'm walking with my new boy-friend."

Thereat the elephant changed its tactics. Going to the other side of the tree, the beast stood beneath the man, and, applying its trunk to the tree trunk, began pulling downward with all its strength. The tree, already very much loosened at the roots, could not long withstand the weight of such a huge animal.

But Scarface, coolly leaning down until his arm was within reach of the beast's trunk if it had seen fit to release its hold on the tree, blazed away all seven shots of his automatic, square at the center of the high flat forehead, which now constituted such a point-blank target.

Stunned, the mammoth recoiled on its haunches for an instant; then flung itself at the tree in a frenzy of rage. The shots must have missed the brain, which in these prehistoric elephants occupied but a very small part of the massive skull.

The tree was now swaying like a reed, but Scarface calmly inserted another clip, steadied himself with his left hand, and blazed away again, this time at the two little red eyes of hate that glared up at him.

Again the impact of the forty-fives stunned the beast and forced it back upon its haunches. And again it returned to its onslaught against the tree. But this time, totally blinded, it missed the tree completely, and went dashing off across the plain.

Dropping with a grunt of relief from the well-nigh horizontal tree, Scarface unslung his rifle, knelt, and discharged all five shots of his magazine at the departing animal; but, unaffected by his shots, it disappeared into the woods which lined the plain.

Scarface, exasperated, brushed off his soiled and disarranged yachting costume, as Mike Murphy, Tom Jones and Little Arty dropped one by one from neighboring trees.

From the air above them rang out a silvery laugh. All four looked up. Over the edge of the cliff-top, they saw a face, at each side of which an ash-blond braid hung down over the rocks.

Scarface doffed his hat, and blew a kiss to the lady from his finger-tips. The face promptly disappeared.

"It's hard to tell at this distance, but I think she's a pippin," remarked Little Arty.

"I believe that that must be the Swede girl that I've always dreamed of meeting some day," announced the handsome young gang leader.

"Good luck to you, Romeo," chimed in Tom Jones.

"That's all very well," said Murphy, "but how do we get up there, anyhow?"

"We holler, I guess," replied Scarface, and suited the action to the word.

But the cliffs above might just as well have been barren, uninhabited rocks for all the effect that their shouting developed, then or later. They separated to circle the plateau.

THEY met again, two meals later, at their starting point, without any of them being able to report any progress. Accordingly they withdrew for another "night" of turns at watching and sleeping.

Finally rested, they ate breakfast—the last that was left of their compressed rations—and then decided that some change of tactics was imperative if they would rescue Terry. So they set out to the southward along the trail which they had seen taken by the Vikings who had left the plateau two days ago. In this way they hoped either to reach wherever the Vikings might be bound, or to meet them coming back.

The trail led sometimes through tangled forests and sometimes through open plains. The central sun beat pitilessly down, and aloft in the heavy air circled one huge and solitary leather-winged *skwaa*, in search of carrion. After several hours, hunger began to gnaw at them, and the circling *skwaa* took on a menacing aspect.

A bit further on, a long-legged rabbit-like creature suddenly appeared in the trail ahead of them. All four rifles blazed simultaneously, and the little creature fell.

"Bedad, we eat!" exclaimed Murphy.

"Let's carry it till we come to water," suggested Tom.

They had not gone far, when they came to a grove of gigantic orange-trees beside a little river which crossed their path at right angles. There they halted and built a fire, and soon the little animal, skinned, dressed, and spitted, was sizzling savorily over the crackling flames.

After the meat, they peeled and divided one monster orange, and reclined, their backs against trees, eating the segments as though they had been huge slices of watermelon.

A cool breeze blew through the little grove. The brook tinkled merrily over its pebbles. The moss which covered the ground beneath the trees was thick and comfortable. Large green and blue and silver butterflies fluttered lazily about in the shafts of crimson sunlight that fell through the openings in the leafy canopy. The four men were replete, and would have been completely at peace with the world, if it had not been for their thoughts of little Terry.

But their rifles lay handy, Scarface's across his knees, for they hadn't yet forgotten the elephant episode.

"Not a bad meal at all," mused their dark curly-haired leader, rising to his feet. "There is not an eating-joint in the States could beat it."

"*Staap!*" came a challenging shout from across the stream.

Murphy leaped erect. Tom and Little Arty rushed back for their rifles. On the other bank of the stream stood two Vikings, with weapons alert.

NOW THAT the first moment of surprise was over, Scarface threw his rifle into the crotch of his left elbow, where it was handy, but not threatening and holding his right hand aloft in what he had read somewhere was a gesture of friendship, he said: "We've been looking for you—"

"*Yee forstaar ikka,*" replied one of the Norsemen.

"I guess you're right," agreed Jimmy, advancing with his friendliest smile. "Now the idea is—"

But the Vikings motioned him back and brandished their spears menacingly. Jimmy halted and frowned, then held up his rifle and pointed to it. He could be threatening, too, if the occasion demanded. How absurd they were, these men out of the past, to dare to match their puny spears and swords against Springfield rifles and Colt automatics! Well, they ought to know what firearms were, from their experience with Eric and Angus.

This gave him an idea.

"Eric Redmond. Angus Selkirk," he pronounced clearly and distinctly.

"*Yah! Yah!*" replied the Norsemen, their expressions indicating that they now realized that these four strangers were compatriots of the two young Americans which he had named.

Jimmy's three henchmen now stood at his side. And more Vikings had joined those on the opposite bank of the stream. But still both parties hesitated to make further overtures.

At this moment a glad girlish cry broke from the thicket behind the Vikings.

"Yoo-hoo, Mr. Jimmy," she cried. "Gee, but I'm glad to see you again."

And Theresa Ferreira bounded onto the scene.

With this introduction, the Vikings signalled to the Americans that they might cross, and soon Theresa was delightedly hugging her former comrades, much to their present embarrassment.

"Terry!" exclaimed Tom fervently.

"Where did you come from? And how do you happen to know these men?" inquired Scarface.

"It's a long story. I ducked out from the wop, and these squareheads picked me up," said the girl. "Tell you all about it in a minute."

Then the Vikings warmly shook hands with the four Americans.

"Isn't this better, Scarface," asked Tom, when they secured a moment's breathing space, "than to shoot down these fine fellows and try to steal their country away from them?"

But Scarface Boston Jimmy reserved his opinion on that subject. In spite of his reading and the superficial culture that had won him the half derisive, half respectful title of "Boston" Jimmy, he was at heart a Chicago gangster.

Suddenly Terry looked around her with puzzled bewilderment.

"But where's father?" she asked.

"You poor child," replied Scarface, putting his arm protectingly across her shoulders. "Your father is dead. He was shot in the fight for the *Miami*."

Theresa burst into tears.

"The thing to do," suggested Scarface gently, "is to get your friends to back-trail and help me recover possession of our boat."

"Yeah?" said she, smiling through her tears. "But how are we going to tell it to them? Can any of you talk Viking?"

CHAPTER X

GUESTS OR PRISONERS?

IT WAS, INDEED, a task for superhuman ingenuity to attempt to explain to the Norse warriors that there was a gasoline yacht somewhere to the southward, and that repossession of that boat was of vital importance. You can't make gestures indicative of a motor boat; and to say *"Phut-phut-phut!"* means nothing to a person who has never heard a motor.

After scratching his head for a few minutes in perplexity, Scarface Jimmy took a piece of dead wood, and whittled out a rough model of a canoe, while the Vikings suppressed their impatience at his apparently childish occupation, and maintained a polite semblance of interest.

Placing the completed craft in the water of the little brook, "Boat," said he.

"Yah, boat," replied the young leader of the warriors. Evidently the Norse word was very much like the English, though the sound was very much flatter.

Meanwhile, under Jimmy's direction, the others of his party had been carving little wooden figures of men. These were now placed in the boat.

"Men in boat," explained the gangster. Then, pointing first to himself and then to the southward, he said, "My boat."

Walking with exaggerated steps to the south, he picked up the boat, hugged it to his breast, and then walked north again.

"Gee, Mr. Jimmy," exclaimed Theresa, laughing in spite of her grief, "they'll think you mean you want to go somewhere, and get some toy boats and wooden dolls to play with."

Arty snickered audibly. Murphy grinned. But Tom Jones and Scarface were deadly serious. However, the blond youth in the chain-mail seemed to catch on—after a fashion.

Holding up one finger, he pointed to the toy boat and to the south. Then holding up one, two, three, four, all fingers, and opening and closing his hand several times, he pointed to the north, beckoned the others to follow him, and resumed the march.

His meaning was obvious: if his guest wanted a canoe, there were plenty to be had at the plateau city; come on! And he strode off to the northward.

"I guess we'll have to wait till we get to the plateau," asserted Tom Jones. "Let's hope one of the two Milwaukee aviators is there to interpret for us. Terry, will you walk with me?"

The girl tossed her head, and replied saucily, "Thanks a lot, Mr. Jones, but I'm walking with my new boy-friend here."

And she ranged herself alongside the mail-clad warrior.

Tom Jones's views on the subject of Vikings underwent a sudden change. Heretofore they had seemed to him to be splendid heroic creatures out of the romantic past. Now they suddenly became crude, rough and untutored savages in his eyes. They really did not "belong." To a Harvard man, this was final!

Dropping back in the line of march to a position beside Scarface Boston Jimmy, he said, "You know, chief, you may be right in your plans to fight these fellows. There may be a chance yet."

Scarface looked long and penetratingly at his young protégé, then glanced ahead at Theresa swinging happily along at the side of the Viking leader, whose hand rested protectingly on her elbow. The gangster smiled understandingly, but said nothing.

THEIR next meal was long overdue ere they reached the plateau, and clambered up, one after the other, through the chimney-like entrance. Their approach must have been noted, for the stone slab had been removed from the top, and a group of tall blond men and women were awaiting them there.

An explanation, in an unknown tongue, ensued among the Vikings, with much pointing at their five guests—or prisoners.

Then one of the Vikings ordered, *"Komm!"*

Something in the way in which this man included her with her four male companions caused Theresa to realize suddenly that these Vikings all regarded her as a little boy. And why not, when it had taken the gangsters so long to discover the secret of her true sex!

This put an entirely different light on the interest which the young chieftain in chain-mail had shown in her. He had just been big-brotherly, that was all. The idea!

Theresa promptly determined to right the matter at once. Walking over to a group of women, she pointed to herself and then to them. But they misunderstood her and shooed her away. Then she made a motion with both hands around her legs to indicate a skirt, pretended to do up her closely-cropped hair in a pug, and pointed to herself.

Her four fellow-countrymen nodded their heads vigorously and waved her away. This time the women got the idea, and led Theresa off with them, while the men led Scarface, Tom, Mike and Arty away to a house, where they were fed, and given blankets and wooden benches to sleep on.

This did not at all suit Scarface. The lack of communication between Shim and his hosts—or captors—was getting on his nerves, as was the delay in taking steps to recover possession of the *Miami,* and to thwart whatever diabolical plans Nick the Rat might have in mind. The fact that, as soon as Scarface regained the gasoline-yacht, his own plans might become just as diabolical as Nick's, did not seem to him to be in the least inconsistent.

"Say, don't any of you speak English?" he asked. "I want to see Angus Selkirk or Eric Redmond at once! Do you get me? Angus Selkirk! Eric Redmond! At once! Now! Immediately! *Pronto!* What's the Swede for 'quick?'"

"*Yah, yah, yarl, imorgen,*" replied one of the Vikings.

"Sounds to me for all the world like a college yell," Scarface remarked to Tom. "Say, you're a college man. What do you make out of it?"

"Well," replied Jones dubiously, " '*Yah*' means 'yes,' and '*yarl*' means 'earl,' the title held by Eric and Angus. So the other funny word must mean when they are going to let us see one of them. Sounded like *Morgen,* the German for 'to-morrow.' I guess we'll just have to wait until that time comes, whenever it is."

"Then let's turn in," said Scarface, resignedly.

"I wish they was a radio here," grumbled Little Arty.

"I believe this is a jail," asserted Mike Murphy. "That bird you were just talking to is the spitting image of one of the deputy sheriffs of Suffolk County."

THE NEXT morning they were ushered out of the building. Theresa was waiting outside, with several of the Viking women. But such a different Theresa! Gone was her natty sailor costume, and in its place she wore the same sort of clothing as the women about her. Her boyish bob didn't quite fit; but, for all that, she looked very regal for such an impudent little sprite.

"Gee, Mr. Jimmy," she greeted them, "will you look at the clothes! These ladies took away all my own things, so I had to put on these. Do they look awful?"

"Not at all bad," admired Tom earnestly.

But she ignored him with a toss of her head, and continued, "You know those kind of things you clean sinks with? Made up of lots of little iron rings hitched together?"

"I never cleaned any sinks," replied Scarface, amused but a bit puzzled as to the point of her remarks, "but I think I know what you mean."

"Well you know that boy, who had the shirt made out of that same kind of stuff? The boy I walked with?"

Tom Jones scowled unhappily.

Terry went on, "Well, I saw him again this morning, and him and me got along fine. We couldn't talk much, but I told him my name was Theresa Ferreira, and then he pointed to himself and said, 'Nils Uppri.'"

"What?" gasped Scarface and Tom in unison.

"Say that again," Tom demanded.

"Nils Uppri," she repeated. "What of it? Ain't that a nice enough name?"

"Sure it's a nice enough name," replied Scarface, "only it happens to be the name of the bishop of all this country. Nils Uppri! What do you know about that?"

It was now Terry's turn to be surprised.

"A bishop!" she exclaimed, her lip curling scornfully. "The dirty pup! A priest, making up to a poor girl like me. He'd oughta known better. I ask you, Mr. Murphy, is it right?"

"It sure don't sound right to me," asserted the Irishman, shaking his head. Then brightening, "But perhaps he's an Episcopal bishop. Sure, that would be a fine match for ye, Terry."

"No such thing," asserted Tom, "It's a dirty trick for him to—"

"You're all wrong!" explained Scarface Jimmy. "Bishops in this country are like kings. The title descends from father to son. Nils Uppri is Bishop, merely because his father, Thorvald Uppri, was the Bishop. And so on, clear back to Eric Uppri, first Christian Bishop of Greenland."

"I don't care what they're like," stated Theresa, pouting, "Bishops oughtn't to marry, and that's all there is to it."

"Did he ask you to marry him?" asked Scarface in surprise.

"No, he didn't. That is— Oh, I don't know what you're talking about, I think you're perfectly horrid." And Theresa blushed violently.

"Gee!" whistled Little Arty expressively.

"You shut up!" snapped Tom, to Arty's great astonishment.

Just then one of the Vikings relieved the situation by saying, "*Komm!*"

As they followed him, the girl remarked, half to herself, "Perhaps he isn't a bishop, after all."

THEY were led to a large building, which seemed to be a sort of assembly hall. In it, benches were arranged as in a church, and these were occupied by groups of warriors chatting together in a low tone of voice. At the end where the pulpit should have been, there was a long carved wooden table, with several high-backed chairs behind it.

The center chair, with the highest back, was occupied by a tall broad-shouldered Viking, with sandy locks and a massive red beard. On his right sat the young leader of the expedition which had brought them hither. The other chairs were vacant.

Scarface, Theresa, Tom, Mike and Arty were led down the aisle to a position facing the Vikings seated at the table. As their conductor bowed low before these Vikings, the Americans did likewise; but there was something unconsciously regal in the courteous bow of Scarface.

The red-bearded Viking, his poker-face inscrutable, studied each of them in turn with his gray-blue eyes.

Then said he, in excellent English, "Who are you and what are you doing in our country?"

Was it possible that this dignified and authoritative Norse warrior could be one of the two young Milwaukee aviators, Eric and Angus? It seemed hardly likely. And yet could they, in so short a time, have taught such perfect English to one of the Vikings? That was equally unlikely.

"And whom have we the honor of addressing?" replied Scarface.

The Viking frowned as he said, "A bad beginning, my friend. But I will tell you. I am Angus Selkirk, formerly of Milwaukee, and now a *yarl* among these Greenlanders. And you?"

Scarface assumed his most disarming and engaging smile.

"We are honored," said he. "For three days we have been trying to get in touch with either you or Eric Redmond on a matter of vital importance, to us all. My name is James Lefavour of Chicago. May I present Miss Theresa Ferreira of Edgartown, Mass.; Mr. Thomas Jones, Harvard, 1929; Sergeant Michael J. Murphy, formerly of the Cambridge police; and Mr. Arthur Doe of Chicago."

"And the important matter?" prompted Selkirk, unimpressed.

"We came to your country in a seventy-five-foot motor yacht, after being blown into the polar ice in a storm," continued Scarface. "There has been mutiny aboard our ship, and fighting between the two factions, each losing one man. At present the ship is in the hands of a thoroughgoing scoundrel, named Nick Fratelli, with four other thugs" (Scarface did not yet know of the death of Scutari) "and one Chinaman. They have practically all the arms and ammunition, including two machine guns."

"Hm," ruminated the Scot. "And how did ye happen to be associating with such rascals?"

CHAPTER XI

DEFIANCE

LITTLE ARTY SNICKERED. The question was, indeed, a poser. But Scarface met it squarely.

Said he, "I am a former Chicago bootlegger, better known as Scarface Boston Jimmy. You may have read about me in the Milwaukee papers, before you came down to this country."

Angus nodded, but did not change expression.

Jimmy continued, "I had read about you in the *Argosy*. So when I found myself blown through the polar opening, I headed for your city, bent on conquest. Frankly, I planned to make myself king, or emperor, or bishop, or whatever you call it, over your Vikings. But I couldn't control my own men, so here I am. I am not asking any favors. I have come to offer cooperation in recapturing the boat; and I never double-cross. However much I may be personally to blame for turning this menace loose on you, the fact remains that the menace exists and must be met at once, or Nick the Rat will succeed in conquering you as I had meant to do."

"Your frankness does you credit," replied Angus Selkirk grimly, "but why should I temporize with such a scoundrel as you admit yourself to be? Why not put you and your three gangsters here to death, and then go after the rest of your gang and boat?"

"You can't do it!" announced Scarface, unperturbed.

"Can't put you to death?" sneered Angus. "Don't you realize that it is a *yarl* of the Vikings that you are addressing? I have power of life and death over all prisoners."

"I wasn't talking about your killing me," retorted their prisoner, "Go ahead and do it, if you're that foolish. I meant you can't buck Nick Fratelli and the machine guns. And as for your being an earl, that doesn't impress me in the least. Come down off your high horse. You're nothing but a young Milwaukee newspaper reporter, off on a lark; and you know it, if you'll only stop and think for a moment."

"Enough!" thundered Angus, rising to his feet and drawing his sword.

But Scarface held up his hand in protest.

"Just a moment," said he. "There's no use in getting excited, just because I tell you a few plain facts. You need me worse than I need you, and I'm here to bargain with you, not to listen to threats. What do you suppose I surrendered to your gang for, if not to help you? No one was after me."

Angus sank back in his seat, amazement taking the place of his wrath.

"Well, of all the colossal nerve!" he exclaimed. "You are dragged before me, unarmed and a prisoner, and then you try to tell me where I get off! All right, proceed. Tell me."

"Now you're talking!" replied Scarface. "I thought you'd listen to reason. The situation is simply this: I know the *Miami,* and her equipment, and the personality of every one of her scoundrelly crew. They have a hundred rifles aboard. Two machine guns. Ample ammunition. They can clean your whole Viking civilization off the map. They have no morals, and no scruples."

"Have you?" interjected Angus pointedly.

"We'll let that wisecrack pass," returned Scarface suavely. "The point is that I understand the enemy, and will know when and where to find their weak spots. Tom Jones here is a scientific expert, who will be a valuable asset to your civilization. Little Arty is a radio hound, who may come in handy at any moment. And Mike Murphy is a scrapping Irish policeman, totally without fear. We offer you our services."

"And the price?" inquired Angus; who had by now completely recovered his composure. "That is, I assume you are demanding your freedom as the price."

"Our freedom?" laughed the gangster. "If that was all we wanted, why did we give ourselves up, in the first place? I demand an earldom for myself, and lands and some sort of rank for each of my three loyal men."

"**I RATHER** like you," replied the red-bearded *yarl*, ruminatively. "You've got such a colossal nerve! A prisoner, not begging some slight favor in return for his services, but rather demanding a yarldom. This is rich! And the joke is that you'll probably succeed in bluffing us into giving it to you. For the present you may consider yourself on probation. You may dismiss your followers and discuss details with Bishop Uppri and ourself."

"Gee, Mr. Yarl," interjected Theresa, "is that boy a real bishop?"

"Yes, madam," replied Selkirk.

"Then will you please tell him in Swedish for me that I've got a new boy-friend?" said she, and walking over to Tom Jones she placed her hand confidingly in his arm.

Tom squared his shoulders and glowered belligerently at Nils Uppri. The latter needed no translation of the message. Although he couldn't fathom the reason, he sensed the purport from Theresa's action. So he smiled sadly down on her and shook his head.

Then Tom, Theresa, Mike, and Arty withdrew. The *yarl* motioned Scarface to a seat at the council table, and the two, with the young bishop, engaged in a discussion of terms and plans.

With continued frankness, the gangster sketched for them the entire story of his adventures. From time to time, Angus translated to Nils.

Finally Scarface concluded with: "Any questions?"

"Yes," replied Nils Uppri through his interpreter, "Why does not the girl like me any more?"

Angus burst into brief laughter. Then in translating this to the gangster, he added, "I think that I can answer that question myself. In our America, Mr. Lefavour, as you know, a Catholic bishop is a priest, and priests are celibates. Is that it?"

"That's the way I size it up," agreed Scarface.

"Well, it's perfectly preposterous! For a person of Nils Uppri's high station to consider that little gutter-cat."

"I don't know," ruminated the gangster, " 'A cat may look at a king,' so why not at a Viking bishop? But, seriously speaking, I saw the boy's face—his reverence's face, I mean, or whatever you call him—when you gave him her message, and it certainly showed some concern. Also, his first question after I told my story just now, about the girl, rather than about the menace which threatens his people. Don't be too hasty, Mr. Selkirk; he seems pretty much of a love-struck lad."

Which comment Angus did not include in his translation to Nils.

THEN the discussion reverted to the problem as to what were Fratelli's probable plans, and as to where he was likely to strike first. So intently were they weighing every possibility, that they did not notice the lady who came and stood beside them.

Presently she spoke in soft Norse, "Angus, dear, we have just heard from Helga on the air. She is setting out at once to visit us, taking advantage of a supply-ship which happens to be sailing to-day."

The three men looked up. Jimmy's scar flared red for an instant, for this was the beautiful girl who had smiled down at him from the plateau, just after he had driven off the mammoth. But Angus too was looking at her, and so did not see the gangster's confusion. Jimmy had not understood her words, but something in her tone of voice in addressing Angus, warned Jimmy to school his features; so that, when Angus turned toward him, his face was again expressionless.

"My dear," said the Scot in Norse, "May I present a fellow-countryman of mine, Mr. Lefavour." Then in English, "Mr. Lefavour, this is my wife, Astrid.

"Please excuse her intrusion. She came to tell me that her sister, Helga—Mrs. Eric Redmond, you know—is about to come here from our southern city on a visit."

As she turned and faced the gangster, a violent red flush mantled her features, for she recognized the man at whom she had smiled a few days ago. But her husband was facing the gangster, and so did not notice her blush. It was all that Scarface could do to maintain his composure under Angus's scrutiny.

So this girl, with whom he had flirted, was another man's wife! Was, in fact the wife of the most powerful man in this community, the man whose good will it was most essential for him to win. Well, if fate should ever give him back his gang, and his ship, and his guns and ammunition the fact that she was another man's wife, or whose wife she was, might not make so much difference after all! While there's life, there's hope.

He would be careful what he promised Selkirk, now. For the present, the important thing was to distract Angus Selkirk's attention, before he noticed their confusion.

So said Scarface, "Suppose the ship, which carries Mrs. Redmond, should run afoul of Nick the Rat in the *Miami*. What then?"

"Hell's delight!" exclaimed the *yarl*. "We must get her on the air and call the trip off. Come on."

He gathered up his gown and hurried not very dignifiedly from the hall. Astrid and Scarface followed him, side by side, tense and self-conscious, while Nils Uppri, the boy bishop, brought up the rear.

Angus led the way to his castle, one of the more pretentious of the dwellings of the little community, a rude structure of hand-hewn timber and hand-fitted stone, furnished inside with a queer mixture of barbaric Norse splendor, Scotch simplicity, and Yankee ingenuity. The American note was distinctly pre-dominant.

In the main hall, or living-room, was the radio set which had formerly graced the polar airplane of the two Milwaukee explorers. The generator, which formerly had been run by the motor of the plane, was now operated by a series of wooden wheels and leather belts, manipulated by one of the *yarl's* Skraeling slaves.

Immediately on their arrival the slave was called, and the machinery was started turning. But for some reason, the apparatus failed to send.

Angus frantically tested here and there with voltmeter and ammeter, plied with pliers, and screwed with screwdriver; but still the thing wouldn't work.

THE INCONGRUITY of an ancient Viking nobleman, in the Milwaukee type living-room of a barbaric castle, broadcasting in the Norse language into a radio set powered by crude wooden wheels and a Skraeling slave, in the presence of a Viking princess, the Bishop of Greenland, and a Chicago gangster, was not lost on Scarface.

He grinned broadly, in spite of the seriousness of the situation, as he offered the services of Tom and Arty. Angus said a few words in Norse to Astrid, who promptly left the room, to have the men summoned. A few minutes later she returned, and a younger girl with her, their arms twined together. Except for age, they were as alike as two peas.

Scarface gasped. He had thought Astrid beautiful, but this new girl was even more lovely, and with greater youth. The girl smiled shyly, almost roguishly at him, as though she knew some secret joke about him. Scarface smiled back. He was naturally a prepossessing young man, and looked well in his natty yachting costume.

"Lefavour—Borghild," introduced Astrid, with a quaint intonation.

"Oh, yes," chimed in Angus, looking up from his machinery, "Mr. Lefavour, this is my wife's cousin, Borghild Hoglund. I guess Astrid has already told Borghild about you."

And he resumed his work.

An awkward pause ensued, not broken until the arrival of Tom Jones and Little Arty. Tom glowered at the bishop. Then he and Arty fell to work on the radio.

In a short time the latter had spotted the trouble, and had repaired it. The generator again began to hum, and Angus called for his friend Eric's station in the southern city, while Nils, Astrid, Tom and Arty crowded around the set, and Scarface and Borghild smiled silently at each other.

But, at that moment in the southern city, Yarl Eric Redmond was down at the wharf seeing his wife off on her trip north, and so his station did not answer. The warning to Helga, to beware of Nick Fratelli, could not be delivered.

CHAPTER XII

THE FATAL WARNING

BY THE TIME Angus Selkirk had learned of the danger that Helga Redmond might fall into the clutches of Nick Fratelli and his crew of cutthroats, those gentlemen had returned to the *Miami*, burdened down with their spoils, and dog-weary from their long trek under the hot central sun.

Charley Loy was unshackled and sent to the galley, while Nick called a conference.

"We've gotta find them Skraelings," asserted Fratelli. "This time I'm going to send Friday alone. If we all go, we'll get into a fight with them, just like we did with the Vikings."

So he conferred lengthily with the Eskimo, and put him ashore fully armed and provisioned. To guard against attack, they anchored the *Miami* a short way out into the water. Then they sat down to await Friday's return.

"See if you can't tune in something," suggested Fratelli.

Cicero tried time and again, at Nick's command. Finally, after dinner, he caught a fragmentary word. Juggling the dials in hit-and-miss fashion, he finally got the station again. It was a man's voice, broadcasting in a strange language.

Swede pricked up his ears.

"*Svenska,*" he announced.

Instantly their saturnine chief became interested.

"Swedish, eh? What are they saying?" Nick asked eagerly.

So Swede translated as well as he could, although some of the words were new to him. Angus had at last got the southern

city on the air, and some Viking of the south was now explain-
ing to him that Eric was down at the wharf seeing Helga off.

When the fellow finally summoned Eric to the machine, the
conversation continued, with appropriate pauses in which to
switch over from sending to receiving, and vice versa, and to
stop and start the generator-sets, for they had reverted to this
method, as being simpler than the two-wave-length simultane-
ous sending and receiving formerly employed by them.

The eavesdropping gangsters on the *Miami* learned that
Eric's wife had already gone before the warning arrived, and
they heard the horrified *yarls* describing the *Miami's* crew in
most uncomplimentary terms, as Eric prepared to send a fast
ship post-haste in a desperate attempt to head off Helga's swift
vessel.

Nick gave his subordinates a triumphant grimace. "Right
into our hands!"

WHEN the two *yarls* had signed off, Nick remarked: "Now we
know as much about them as they do themselves, and they don't
know a thing about us. I'll get that little Terry yet. And you and
Swede and Friday, and even the Chink, can have your pick of
the squarehead women. What was it that Napoleon said under
similar circumstances?"

"Now, now, chief," remonstrated Cicero. "Don't get talking
and acting like Scarface. There's only one of that sort, thank
God."

Fratelli glowered, but did not attempt to perpetrate any more
highbrow language.

They were sleeping for the second time since Friday's departure when they were aroused by a commotion on shore. Nick
Fratelli looked out of his porthole.

On the beach there stood about twenty savages, and in their
midst was the Eskimo, his hands tied behind him, his feet
hobbled, and a halter around his neck.

Hastily dressing, Nick, Cicero, and Swede rushed on deck,
fully armed. Charley Loy remained discreetly out of sight.

"What's the trouble?" shouted Fratelli, in Eskimo language.

"These very bad men," replied Friday, "they not believe me."

"Tell them I want to speak to Altoonah, their chief," thundered Fratelli. "Where is he?"

A straight-featured young native, wearing a Viking helmet and a shirt of chain-mail, but supported by crude crutches, hobbled painfully forward.

"I am Altoonah," said he in Norse. "What of it?"

Swede translated to Nick.

"Speak Innuit!" ordered the latter, adding to himself: "It's Altoonah, all right, for the story says he was crippled."

"I am Altoonah," repeated the native chieftain, this time in the native language. "What of it?"

"I seek your alliance to fight the Vikings," replied the gangster. "Did not my man Friday give you that message?"

"He did, but we did not believe him. You are the same race as Eric and the elephant-faced one. You ought to be on their side. So we do not believe you. It is a trap."

"It is *not* a trap!" boomed Nick. "Positively not."

"What is your grievance against the Vikings?" asked Altoonah.

"None," answered Fratelli. "We seek conquest."

"Ho! I begin to believe you," said the Skraeling. "If you were lying, you would have invented some grievance. Then what will you offer for our help? For we, too, have no grievance against the Vikings. And *we* desire no conquest."

Of course, the conversation did not go quite so smoothly as this, for Nick Fratelli was new at the Eskimo language, and some of the Skraeling words differed from those which he had learned from Friday, but the foregoing was the substance of what was said.

"How about Helga Uppri?" asked the gangster, pausing to let his words sink in. He had read of Altoonah's vain attempts to win the girl who was now Eric Redmond's wife.

The native's face became purple with rage. He shook one crutch at the man on the deck.

"Who dares taunt Altoonah?" he shouted.

"No one taunts you," soothed Nick. "I offer you friendship and help. Helga is at this moment on her way north in one Viking ship. She shall be yours, if you will assist me in my plans."

Eagerness replaced the wrath on the Skraeling's face, but one of his followers stepped to his side and spoke in low tones to him, quite evidently urging him not to believe the treacherous foreigners.

Nick spoke in Johnson's ear. The Swede's rifle cracked, and the adviser of the Skraeling chief dropped to the ground without a sound.

Before any other feeling than surprise had had time to develop, Fratelli bellowed forth: "Who else wishes to lie to Altoonah, to try and turn him against his good friend?"

There were no takers. Altoonah held up his hand as a sign of amity, and released Friday. Altoonah and his party came on board. Noting that the chief was dressed in imitation of the Vikings, and that his features betokened a high degree of intelligence, the gangster did not offer him gaudy handkerchiefs, or the like, the sort of present which had won Friday, the Eskimo. Instead, he gave him the sword and belt and scarf-buckle, which he had taken from one of the dead Vikings.

CHAPTER XIII

A VIKING AIR RAID

BETWEEN THE PERIL of Helga Redmond, and the mystery of the overlong absence of the Viking scouting party— the five warriors who had been ambushed by Nick Fratelli's crew—there was great uneasiness and considerable activity in the plateau city.

A new and stronger scout patrol was dispatched, its strength greatly augmented by the armed presence of Jones, Murphy, and Little Arty.

Theresa had begged to go; and the request had brought from her hostess, Astrid, the single word *"Valkyr!"* It was pronounced with such horror that Terry blurted hastily to Angus: "Gee, Mr. Selkirk, I ain't that kind of girl, really!"

The young bishop and Angus requested Scarface to remain with them to plan their campaign, and he gladly accepted. He had already decided to add the Norse language to his accomplishments, and Borghild, the beautiful, volunteered to teach him.

So the expedition set forth, and in due course of time came upon the stripped and desecrated bodies of the five Viking dead and of the gangster Scutari. Two of the party were placed on guard, and a runner was dispatched back to the plateau with the news.

A little further on they ran into the pack of hyænodonts that had been following Nick Fratelli and his gang. Five of the dog-beasts they killed, to lay at the feet of the five warriors when given Viking burial, this being the chief use made of these fierce denizens of the woods; in fact, they were protected by Viking law, and not permitted to be slain except for this purpose or in self-defense.

When the runner reached the plateau, there was consternation there. Angus conferred with Scarface.

"We must get word to the scouts at once by glider," announced Angus, "instructing them to locate the gangsters and await reënforcements. Perhaps if we strike suddenly enough, we may overpower Fratelli's crew in spite of their weapons, for they are as yet very few.

"Would you like to make the flight in our new two-seated glider? We plan to drop the note of instructions to the scouting party, then try to locate the enemy from the air, and then drop a second note, informing our scouts of the enemy position. You can write this second note, and your three men, even if they cannot translate it to my troops, can at least lead the way by following your directions."

Scarface was tempted by the thought of Borghild, but the prospect of action, and the novelty of a glider-flight proved too strong, so he gladly assented.

"Of course, in such a long flight, you may be forced down," added Angus, "for these motorless planes are very tricky. But you can reach one of our parties, and have them guard the glider, disassemble it and ship it back."

"How do these things work?" inquired Scarface, now showing much interest; and he added:

"I've read about your flying experiences, but I never could quite figure how you did it. It's all very well to talk about taking advantage of shifts of wind and of every up-current of air, but why don't these shifts and up-currents come upon you too suddenly for you to take advantage of them?"

Angus Selkirk smiled indulgently.

"**WE'VE LEARNED** a lot since Astrid, Helga, Eric and I built our first gliders out of *skwaa*-skin and split bamboo, when the Skraelings besieged us on this plateau. In those days we trusted largely to luck, and took the air-currents as they came. But since then we have made quite a study of meteorology, and have found that the gusts obey regular rules. By watching the ground and the clouds, we can tell just about what to expect and where to expect it.

"For example, we expect strong up-currents directly under clouds, and diffused down-currents just beyond their edges. We expect up-currents over plains; down-currents over woods, and even stronger ones over water. Near the ground the air is apt to rush in toward woods and water, while at higher levels the drift is just the opposite. If the wind is blowing toward a hill, it rises at the hill; if away, it falls.

"So, by watching the ground and the sky, we know what to expect, and are prepared to take advantage of it. But mostly we have learned the 'feel' of the air. We fight the air automatically, just as a boxer or a fencer fights his opponent."

"Have you any theory to explain these air-currents?" asked Scarface.

"Yes," replied the Scotch Viking. "We think that they are due to the sun's heating the earth unequally, owing to differences in soil. Hot air rises, cold settles. Clouds are warmed by the sun, and their under side remains cool.

"We imagine that these phenomena are much more regular down here than on the outer surface of the earth, due to the fixed position of our central sun. But in both places they probably exist to a much greater extent than is dreamed of. They furnish the only possible explanation of how we are able to soar and gain height on calm days, with scarcely a trace of wind."

"Yes," confirmed Scarface, "I saw in the papers, shortly before leaving the outer earth, that gliders had actually stayed aloft in Germany for over eight hours."

"We have almost equaled that record here," asserted Angus proudly.

This conversation made Scarface all the more anxious to try one of these strange motorless planes.

SCARFACE said good-by—Angus giving him the words—to Borghild, and warmly pressed her hand. He took his automatic and all his .45-caliber clips—his rifle having been loaned to the leader of the reënforcing party. Then the glider was wheeled to the edge of the plateau, he was introduced to the young Viking aviator named Oskar Hiher; the two took their seats, and the machine was pushed off into space.

Oskar proved to be most expert. He slid and circled and spiraled, taking advantage of every shift in wind, every stratum and cross-current of air, always working higher and always tending southward.

In a very few minutes, it seemed, they passed over the sentries guarding the Viking dead, and then passed over the advance party, still pressing on down the trail. The message was dropped, and the glider kept on.

From their height, the *Miami* was soon spotted in the distance.

"Boat," said Scarface, pointing.

"*Yah, boat,*" replied the aviator.

Then reaching into a pouch beside him, he produced several round objects about the size of oranges.

"*Bomma,*" said he.

"*Yah,* bombs!" replied Scarface.

There were some things that they could mutually understand, in spite of their difference in language. The two men grinned at each other. Eight hundred years apart in race and customs, and the whole earth's crust apart in environment, nevertheless they were brothers under the skin.

Bombs! This was going to be fun! Scarface reached for one, but his companion shook his head and tapped his forehead. The meaning was plain: Scarface lacked the necessary air experience.

They arrived over the *Miami* at quite a height. The conference with Altoonah was still in progress, although that gentleman was not in evidence. There were, however, plenty of Skraelings on deck, and their relations with Swede and Friday were evidently friendly.

"*Skraelingna,*" announced Oskar, and Scarface began writing his report, stating that Nick and the Skraelings had already contacted, and were probably concocting an alliance.

No one on board seemed to notice the plane. Perhaps they mistook it for a large *skwaa*.

Circling to the southeast, the glider passed over a body of Skraelings on the march toward the coast. Some of these noticed the glider, and soon they were called to the attention of the whole party. This would never do. These savages would get in touch with the *Miami*, and ambush the Viking foot-parties.

Evidently the same thoughts were simultaneously passing through Oskar's head, for he asked hopefully, "*Bomma?*"

But Scarface shook his head. If they committed no act of hostility against these natives, the report of the natives, on reaching the *Miami*, would lack certainty as to whether the Vikings suspected their plans.

So Scarface shook his head and said, "*Nein.*"

That might not be the proper Viking word for "no," but he had already learned, when in doubt in speaking to a Norseman, to use the German word if he happened to know it.

The plane wheeled back toward the *Miami* again.

"*Skal yee bomma boaten?*" inquired the young Viking. Scarface sensed his meaning.

Why not bomb the boat? Strike before the alliance was formed. Disable the craft and its defenders, so that it might fall a prey to the scouting expedition, shortly to arrive; put an end to the war before it got fairly started. Why not?

"*Yah!*" shouted Scarface Boston Jimmy.

Down out of the sky swooped the glider with a rush, straight toward the *Miami*. The Skraelings on deck scattered, perhaps not realizing that this huge man-made bird was not a *skwaa*, but fearing nevertheless the swoop of so large a pterodactyl.

AS THE glider barely skimmed the roof of the vessel, passing neatly under the aërial, between the masts, one of the orange-like objects was let go. It exploded against the side of the deck house with a loud detonation, laid two of the Skraelings writhing on the deck, and blew a huge hole in the deck house. Consternation reigned on the *Miami*.

"Too bad it wasn't further fore or aft," thought Jimmy. "Aft, it might have got the engines, and further forward might have disabled the navigating controls."

But how to explain this to the wild Viking at his side, who knew as little of English as he himself did of Norse?

Under the force of its own momentum, the glider climbed abruptly to quite a height, then turned and swooped down again toward the *Miami*. If there were only some way to explain to the flyer to strike at one of the ends of the ship!

Quite a group were gathering in the bow, and that gave Scarface an idea. His companion might not understand the location of the vulnerable spots in a motor yacht, but he would certainly get the idea of bombing a group of men; so Scarface nudged him and pointed violently toward the group in the bow.

"*Yah!*" said Oskar, and swung the nose of the glider, so as to pass over the men.

In one hand he held his bomb ready to hurl it among them, as he passed over their heads. But he never hurled it.

When he was still at a distance of about two hundred feet, a staccato rattle like that of a pneumatic riveting machine broke out from the bow of the *Miami*, and a rapid succession of small incandescent spots of light, like silver bees, shot whistling beneath them.

"Up! Up!" shouted Scarface, grabbing the joy-stick in the hand of the astonished Viking, and forcing it back against his chest.

Up soared the glider. But, as if it were a hose-stream being played upon them, up too rose the trail of silver bees deliberately to meet them; and, when it met them, the Viking collapsed with a gurgle in his seat.

Scarface still held the stick, and he clung to it like grim death. He felt a tap on the side of his chest, then a warm tingling feeling there, and then a trickle down his side, but still he held on.

He passed beyond the *Miami*, but the clatter of the machine gun continued. Up, up, soared the glider, into a stall, and then a sideslip. Scarface tried to get his feet past the dead body of his companion and onto the foot-controls, to right her. He failed to reach them, but his efforts somehow shifted the weight and accomplished the desired result, for the craft righted and swung southward.

He now pushed the stick gingerly forward, so as to secure a gentle descent, and thus put as much distance as possible between his enemies and himself. Things were going beautifully. In spite of his lack of control of the stabilizer, the glider for some reason kept an even keel. The sound of the machine gun was fading away in the distance.

Scarface was just congratulating himself on his beginner's luck as an aviator, when the plane suddenly without warning went into a spiral nose dive and plunged into the sea.

CHAPTER XIV

PIRACY

ON THE *MIAMI*, Swede was saying to Nick and Cicero, "I tank it vos Yimmy."

"Then why the hell didn't you and Cicero pot him, instead of the Viking?" ejaculated Fratelli disgustedly. "But it couldn't possibly have been Jimmy—he don't know how to fly."

"Beginner's luck," explained Cicero Tony sagely, adding, "But we got the Viking, anyhow."

"Yah, ve got him," assented Swede, but he didn't seem particularly elated about it. He seemed to have a growing fellow-feeling for these tall blond Norsemen.

"Look, there he crashes!" shouted Nick. "Quick, Cicero, the engines! I'll take the wheel."

But though they searched the water, and even the near-by shore, with great care, they found no trace of their former leader. Finally they gave up the search, and returned to their anchorage. Nick Fratelli was elated. His usually sour features glowed.

"Dead, that's a cinch!" he chortled. "This gets rid of the only man in this country with more brains than I got. I'll be the Vikings' king—I'll be their emperor—why, I may even be their Mussolini!"

Following the attack by the glider, Nick, Altoonah and the impromptu interpreter Friday conferred again, while Charley Loy, assisted by several of the Skraelings, prepared a delectable venison stew, of a colossal prehistoric Irish elk, with chopped breadfruit to take the place of both potatoes and chestnuts, and with bits of orange-peel to give it an acid tang.

The result was really a work of culinary art, and was hailed as a great success by the members of both races. Try it, the next time you kill an Irish elk where there are breadfruit in abundance.

Finally the terms of the alliance were concluded, and the bargain was sealed by the two chiefs solemnly clasping hands over a ring, a Viking custom, one of the many copied by the Skraeling chief. They had to use a deck-ring for the purpose, no other sort of large ring being available.

Then all the remaining rifles, about a hundred in number, were unloaded from the hold, and the pick of Altoonah's warriors, who had by this time arrived, were selected as a rifle company, to be trained under the personal instruction of the three gangsters. This rifle company consisted of one hundred and fifty savages, so as to allow for casualties and still keep the strength up to the available number of Springfields.

The picked Skraeling warriors were very proud of having been chosen, and were anxious to try out the rifles at once; but Nick Fratelli knew from World War experience that recruits should not be given firearms until they had mastered at least the rudiments of discipline and squad-movements.

Nick was not worrying about any attack from the Vikings just yet. The Vikings would probably wait for two or three days before sending out a searching party or another glider; and he could count on about three days additional thereafter, before the enemy would arrive on the scene, for he calculated that his present position was three days' march from the plateau.

Given thus the five or six days leeway that he expected, he could whip his new troops into such shape so that, if they did not break and run at the first attack, their hundred rifles, shooting however wild, would be more than a match for the four to six which the Vikings could muster.

The gangster issued rifles and a little ammunition to Altoonah and his bodyguard, more as an evidence of good faith than because they could be expected to know how to use them.

IN THE morning—which of course was marked by no sunrise, but merely by enough of them waking up to disturb and rouse the others—the squads were formed again, and Nick, in the august presence of King Altoonah and his staff, began the superhuman task of making modern soldiers out of a rabble of naked savages. Yet superhuman as it was, it was absolutely essential to his plans of conquest.

According to Nick's calculations, the enemy against whom he was training these men were still in their rocky fortress many miles to the northward; whereas, in actuality, the enemy were almost upon him.

A fairly level bowlder-dotted field bordered the beach, where the Skraeling horde stood, or reclined, or squatted. In the center of the field were drawn up the two ranks of the incipient rifle company. In front of them, in a group, stood Nick the Rat, with Cicero, Swede and Friday. Also Altoonah, the Skraeling chieftain, with his bodyguard. Charley Loy leaned over the ship's rail, an interested spectator.

Nick issued the commands, with explanations assisted by Friday. Altoonah reënforced his authority.

That edge of the field furthest from the sea was backed by a ledge of rocks, lopped by a thicket of small trees; and from this thicket a score or more of hostile eyes took in every detail of the scene below.

Tom Jones, Mike Murphy and Little Arty—for they were among these spies in the thicket—withdrew stealthily out of earshot, and discussed the situation. The Viking commander of the expedition withdrew with them, although of course he could not contribute very much to the discussion.

"Altoonah?" they asked him.

"*Yah,*" he replied, for he had recognized the crutches.

Its forked tongue, large as an outer-world snake, quivered in and out.

Then said Tom, "Nick has made an alliance with the Skraeling king, just as we feared. Nick carries his right arm in a sling. Swede's left hand and Cicero's right shoulder are bandaged. And we found Scutari dead back there. So I guess our five Vikings did some very creditable fighting before they were finally slaughtered by modern firearms. But what is more to the point, these wounds mean that none of the three white men is very formidable with a rifle right now. And none of the three has his rifle with him at the moment. Altoonah and the savages grouped around him have rifles; but, as they must have got them off the *Miami,* I doubt if any of them has the slightest idea how to use them, except possibly Altoonah himself, and he'd have difficulty handling one on crutches. We four have rifles, know how to use them, and are uninjured. Shall we wait for reënforcements, while Nick arms and trains these savages, or shall we sneak back to the edge of the ridge and shoot up the party?"

"The Skraelings will probably attack us, the moment we open fire," answered Murphy. "There are enough of them to overpower us in spite of our guns."

"Yeah?" sneered Little Arty. "Scared of getting nudged by a hunk of lead, are you? Well, if we bump off the wop, and the squarehead, and Cicero, what difference will it make what happens to *us* after that? Where is your nerve, flat-foot?"

"Let's go," said Tom.

"It's okeh with me," the ex-cop, stung, hastened to agree.

"That makes it anonymous," said the little jockey. "Come on."

Turning to the Viking, Tom patted his own rifle, pointed in the direction of the enemy, crooked his finger a number of times, and said brilliantly, "Bang, bang, bang!"

The Viking smiled and nodded.

"*Yah!*" said he.

THE FOUR of them crawled back to the top of the ledge. The positions of the enemy were practically unchanged. Tom pointed out to the Viking the group on which they were to fire first. Then all four drew a careful bead on Nick Fratelli. It seemed inevitable that at least one of them would be sure to bring down their victim.

But at just that moment they, or some of their followers, were glimpsed by one of the Skraelings.

"Vikings!" rang out the cry.

Instantly the scene on the plain below shifted like a kaleidoscope.

Altoonah might not be versed in modern squad-formations, but, in spite of his inheriting the rank from his father Goovah, he could not have held his kingship over the wild hordes if he had not developed an uncanny ability to direct large bodies of men on the field of battle.

A few words of command shouted by him, and his warriors were charging in a body up the slope. Instinctively Tom, Mike, Arty and their ally depressed their muzzles to aim at the coming attack, and only too late realized that they ought to have pulled their triggers at Nick Fratelli before doing so. Back up swung their muzzles. But Nick and his two henchmen and even Altoonah had taken advantage of the respite to drop behind protecting bowlders. Friday had joined the rush of the Skraelings.

The four on the ledge now fired repeatedly into the oncoming mob, but their shots stopped only individuals. Rather than be engulfed, they slowly fell back inland. Their plan having failed, there was no point in their remaining to be massacred.

As the first impetuousness of the Skraeling charge wore off, the savages advanced more cautiously, and this enabled the Vikings to collect their forces and beat an orderly retreat. They knew, which their assailants did not, that they were falling back upon reënforcements.

Altoonah's bodyguard had instinctively dropped their rifles and reverted to their native spears, when the fighting started. Their king alone kept hold of his firearm, and had hobbled after his men as soon as the Vikings had been driven from their position.

Crawling cautiously from behind their protective rocks, the three gangsters recovered the fallen guns, took them back to the ship and passed them up to Charley Loy.

"We really ought to get into this fight," stated Nick, standing on the beach and looking back toward the battle.

"Vy?" asked Swede.

"Well, it's our fight," explained Nick. "If it weren't for these damn' wounds, we could make those crooks eat lead."

"Let's get out of here while the getting is good," suggested Cicero shamelessly.

"I suppose Altoonah really doesn't need any help," ruminated Nick. "He's got enough men to do them Vikings up, in spite of their guns. We ought to be off after Helga Redmond anyhow. You two go on board and get the *Miami* ready to start, while I have a word with Altoonah."

And he lumbered off in the direction of the fighting.

Altoonah was too canny to lead a charge against modern firearms, especially in his crippled condition, so Fratelli found him in the rear directing the attack. In a few hurried words their plans were made.

Altoonah was to turn over the command to a lieutenant, and with nine picked men was to return to the *Miami,* which was then to start south to intercept the ship bearing Helga Redmond. When the Skraelings had annihilated Tom Jones's party of Vikings, the prospective rifle company were to march south along the shore, keeping an eye out for the *Miami.* The rest of the Skraelings were to go into camp and hold off as long as possible any counter-attacking parties of Vikings.

These plans decided on, Altoonah turned over the command and gave the necessary instructions to his lieutenant. Friday was located in the mêlée, and the group went back to the boat, which they found with engines purring, all ready to depart.

SO THEY set out to the southward, and it was not long before they sighted the painted sail and high prow of the Viking freighter, bound north. She was making good headway, under the influence of her oars and a following wind.

As the motor yacht approached, all those on the Viking ship who were neither rowing nor steering, crowded forward to see the strange sight—a boat moving at an unbelievable speed, without either sails or oars. Among the Vikings could be seen a regal young woman, richly dressed, with rich yellow hair.

The *Miami* sped by, then circled, and slowing down her speed to that of the Viking craft, drew up alongside. Nick Fratelli was at the wheel, Cicero at the engines, Swede and Friday at the bow machine gun, and Altoonah, with only his shield and crutches, beside them in the bow. The rest of the Skraelings and Charley Loy were ranged along the deck, aft.

Nick had never felt so short-handed. He needed Cicero both at the engines and to assist Swede with the bow machine gun, where Friday was but a poor substitute. He would have liked to have manned the stern gun, too, but that was out of the question.

Some of the Vikings were nervously fitting arrows to their bows, as Altoonah began the conversation. It was dangerous, coming thus within range of the enemy, but the swish of the oars and the chug of the motor made intercourse impossible out of bowshot, so the chance had to be taken.

"Who is in command?" shouted Altoonah in Norse.

Helga Redmond stepped to the rail and replied, "I, the Princess Helga. What sort of a godless ship is yours, that sails without sails, and rows without oars? Who are you? And come you for peace or for war?"

"We come for peace, most beautiful Helga," answered the Skraeling chieftain. "This boat is the magic ship of the Innuits, which we have built to prove our superiority over your people, who still rely on clumsy sails and oars. Do you not recognize your former lover, the great Altoonah, King of the Innuits? I have come for you, Helga Uppri, as I promised when you married Eric Redmond."

"You are vile," shouted the princess. "If you do not at once withdraw the insult, I shall have you shot, unarmed and a cripple though you be. The wife of Eric Redmond, and the daughter of Thorvald Uppri, is not for any Skraeling scum."

Now it never does to call a Skraeling a "Skraeling," for their word for themselves is "Innuits." "Skraeling" is like the French word for the Germans, namely "Bodies."

Yet Altoonah smiled as he answered, "And Altoonah is not unarmed. You know the magic slingshots which Eric and Angus brought from the mythical land beyond the northern ice? Well, we Innuits have an even greater weapon, which can devastate your entire ship's company at one blast. If you will come peaceably aboard us, we shall spare their lives. Otherwise they die."

Helga's reply was a sharp command, and the twang of many bowstrings, and the hum of many arrows.

CHAPTER XV

WAR TO THE HILT

AS THE STRINGS of Helga's bowmen twanged, Altoonah, with the speed of light, swung his protecting shield in front of himself and his two companions. The arrows clattered harmlessly off it.

"Spare the girl! Fire!" he shouted.

Swede heard and understood. Before the archers could reload, the machine gun was belching flame to a staccato accompaniment.

As Friday fed in the belts of ammunition, Swede swept the stream of bullets along the deck of the Viking ship like the stream of water from a garden hose. One traverse of the deck, and not a person stood alive on it except Helga. Then a sweep back at a slightly lower level, and every rower on the near side slumped in his seat.

Right through the shields, hung along the gunwales, cut the singing bullets, and many of them reached even the rowers on the farther side. The rowing stopped. Quick as a flash, the *Miami* was steered alongside the Viking ship, crunching the oars between the two boats; and then Swede and Friday clambered aboard, followed by Altoonah, agile of arm despite his palsied legs.

But as they came, Helga snatched a jeweled dagger from the gold chain which encircled her waist, and held it aloft, its tip pointed not at the enemy, but at her own breast. Suddenly left alone amid the shambles that had a moment before been her brave and lusty countrymen, what did there remain for her but death? Even death were preferable to captivity with a member of the despised race of Skraelings, king though he was.

But, just as the dagger fell, there stepped to her side four oarsmen, the only ones who still remained alive out of all the carnage. With drawn swords they sprang to defend their princess to the death and one of them snatched the knife from her hand.

Then the automatics of Swede and Friday barked several times, and Altoonah hobbled to the side of the fainting Helga. Every other Viking lay dead or dying.

Altoonah's Skraelings now surged over the side, slit the throats of the wounded, and pillaged the boat, finding amid the loot enough provisions to stock the *Miami* for a month.

Helga's inert form was carried into the cabin by Swede and Friday, and her hands were shackled with the decidedly convenient handcuffs which formerly had belonged to Policeman Murphy. Swede brought water and threw it in the girl's face.

When her senses had thoroughly been restored, she sat up on the couch where they had laid her, and fearlessly faced Altoonah, Swede, and Friday. Fratelli, who had left the boat drifting, had also come to look at the captive.

As Fratelli gazed at her, his eyes narrowed, and the face of Helga Redmond eclipsed that of Theresa Ferreira from his mind. Not that he altogether abandoned his lust for little Terry, but rather he formulated the idea of establishing a harem, as king of this country, and of having Helga as his principal and favorite wife. This, of course, would necessitate getting rid of Altoonah, instead of using him as an ally; but doubtless that slight matter could be arranged, all in due time.

Luckily Altoonah did not catch Nick's look; but Swede did, and it intensified his growing dislike for his boss. Ever since Swede had come in contact with the Norsemen of the interior of the earth's shell, he had felt an ancestral urge calling across the centuries, to draw him closer to these people of his own race and blood. This girl was a Viking and a lady. Swede was a descendant of Vikings, although not exactly a gentleman. Nick the Rat was only scum, according to Swede's views.

It was all right for Altoonah to aspire to the lady's hand, for Altoonah was a king, even though he was a Skraeling and a cripple. But Nick Fratelli was a different matter. Swede began to wish that he had stuck with Scarface Boston Jimmy. Then, in a moment, he was glad he had not, for here he might be of service to one of his own kind. Swede was rapidly turning the clock back eight hundred years.

SOUNDS of confusion were heard on deck outside.

"You guard the skirt, Swede," commanded Fratelli, "while the king and I go out and quiet his Innuits, who seem to be staging a roughhouse. You can understand her lingo. Perhaps you I can pump some ideas out of her that may be of use to us."

When the two allies had left, Swede with as gentlemanly an air as he could muster, began in his native tongue, "Gracious lady—"

Helga jumped, and interjected. "So you are what my Eric calls a Svenska, one of the Vikings of the outside world, like my Eric. That horrid man, who leered at me, looks like a Skraeling, although he wears the clothes of the outer world. So does the man who boarded my ship with you and Altoonah. So does one other whom I saw standing with the native warriors in the stern of your ship during the battle."

She smiled wryly at the word "battle," and went on, "rather, massacre. But you look like a Viking, and your voice sounds like one. Tell me, what are you doing in such evil company? Are you a renegade to your own people?"

Swede listened, enthralled and concerned.

"Gracious lady," he replied in the nearest approach he could make to Norse, "I was not always one of these men. I was born in Sweden."

"Your language is so like that of my Eric when he first came to these lands," said she, "that I am sure you must be a brave and good man like him. What is your name, Viking?"

"Yon Yonson, gracious lady," he replied. "And my life is at your service."

"Then you must get me out of here," she pleaded, "away from those awful men."

By this time, the noise outside had subsided, and Nick and Altoonah reëntered. As they came in, Nick was making some bombastic remark to his ally, and translated it for Swede's benefit.

Said Nick, "I was telling him that one Italian was a match for a hundred Vikings."

It was the wrong time to make a remark like that to Johnson.

"It vos a Swede and a Eskimo did it, though," remonstrated the latter.

"Yeah?" replied Fratelli. "Well, get this: it was an Italian's brains that directed the whole show."

"I tank—" began Swede.

"Shut up," exclaimed Nick. "None of that line now. How are you getting along with the moll?"

"I tank she tell me a lot."

"All right, pump her dry. Then guard the door. When you get too tired, come and wake Cicero to take your place."

The other two withdrew, and soon the engines could be heard throbbing again. At last the boat slowed, orders were given outside with much running to and fro, and the anchor dropped. Footsteps retired aft, and then silence. The victors were resting.

Swede turned to the captive princess and said: "I tank ve go ashore." Then in Swedish, "Oh, excuse me. I talked the wrong language. Every one will be asleep soon. They plan to go north in the morning to join Altoonah's army."

"Then we must flee north," interjected Helga.

"No! South," asserted Swede, surprised at her suggestion.

"Don't you see?" explained Helga. "They know that you know that they are going north. So they will expect us to flee in the other direction. Accordingly, they will pursue us south; and, if we have gone north, we shall escape."

It was too subtle for Yon Yonson. "Maybe so."

IT SEEMED absurd to be sneaking away from the ship in broad daylight. But after an interval the two tiptoed out of the cabin into the mess-room. There Swede paused and scratched his head for a moment, then whispered, "We've got to take a chance on waking them, for we can't go without food and weapons."

So he tiptoed into the bunk room, presently emerging with two rifles, two ammunition belts, two automatic pistols, two packs, and a broad grin.

Leading Helga onto the deck, and handing her all the equipment except one pistol and belt, and the two packs, he signed to her to stand still, and then he sneaked aft to the door of the galley. There he paused and shook his head sadly for a moment; but finally, pulling himself together, he entered. The cause of his hesitation had been that the Chinaman was sitting asleep in a chair tilted back against the wall, directly across the galley from the door.

But Helga and he must have food for their journey. If the Chink made a move, Swede was prepared to ship out his gun, and bind and gag Charley, under threat of death.

The intruder knew exactly where the compressed rations were kept, having often helped Charley in the kitchen. So he quickly filled both knapsacks. But to do so, it was necessary for him to turn his back on the Chinaman.

The moment his back was turned, the slit-eyes of the Oriental opened slightly and took in the scene without the slightest change in expression or any bodily movement.

Some sixth sense must have warned Swede that he was observed, for suddenly he wheeled around from his work, snatching out his automatic as he turned. But some sixth sense must have warned Charley Loy, too, for Swede saw merely the placid benign face of a sleeping Chinaman.

Charley made no further move, and Swede at last departed with both his packs well-filled with provisions, and rejoined Helga on deck. Not a soul stirred as, Swede helping Helga, because of the manacled condition of her hands, they made their way ashore, and to a protecting fringe of trees. As the fugitives disappeared, two slant eyes in a yellow face watched them from one of the portholes of the *Miami*. And then, if any one could have looked at that moment into the ship's kitchen, they would have seen a surprising sight. They would have seen Charley Loy doing a double shuffle dance, with glee writ large on his usually inscrutable face. But, luckily for his reputation as an imperturbable Oriental, no one saw him, for all others on the *Miami* were sound asleep. Then Charley returned to his chair, refolded his hands across his chest, and resumed his interrupted nap.

SWEDE and Helga, having gained the cover of the trees, were proceeding northward along the shore at a rapid pace.

As soon as they had gone about a mile, and thus were presumably out of hearing of the *Miami*, Swede got two large stones from the beach, and bashed the handcuffs between them, until he had freed his companion. Thus ended the eventful career of Mike Murphy's police manacles.

Although the two fugitives were due to have slept at the very time they started forth yet, tired as they were, they did not dare stop until they had struggled on for about eight hours, under the beating central sun. Then they slept, but whether for a few minutes, or a few hours, or a few days, there was no way of telling. The scene and the time of day on which they reopened their eyes were exactly the same as those on which they had closed them.

They had camped beside a little stream, which flowed tinkling to the sea. Now they roused themselves, washed, ate, and hurried on.

A hundred yards or so beyond the brook, the shore made a decided bend inland, so Swede parted the fringe of bushes to get the lay of the land. He found that they were at the tip of the first of two capes which bounded a harbor about a mile long and half a mile across at the mouth.

The opposite shore was devoid of trees, and there he saw what startled, but did not surprise him—a body of about a hundred and fifty Skraelings on the march south. Hastily withdrawing his head, he informed Helga that Altoonah's newly-formed rifle corps were about to arrive on the scene, on their way to rejoin the *Miami*.

Being a city man, he had no plans. There were here no alleys, down which to duck; no vacant lots to cross; no cellars, in which to hide.

Finally Helga suggested, "Let's hurry back to the little brook, and then go inland in the shelter of the trees and bushes of its ravine."

The idea seemed a good one, so they hastened to put it into execution. Fortunately their progress was assisted by a well-marked animal-trail which paralleled the stream.

As the path ascended, they more and more often caught glimpses of the enemy, until it became evident that, if they went much farther, they would by the same token be in more and more frequent danger of being seen themselves. Besides they were breathless from the speed with which they had made the ascent. So they sat down in the concealment of some bushes, to watch until the enemy should have passed by.

Now the two fugitives saw the *Miami* steam into sight from the southward. It anchored at the mouth of the little brook at whose headwaters Helga and her Swedish protector were hiding, and Fratelli made contact with his Skraeling rifle company. Nick had reasoned, as Helga had expected, that the fugitives had headed south. But she had not foreseen that he would do what he did—steam south, land a search party to work northward and thus head them off, while he sailed the yacht back to meet his rifle corps.

CHAPTER XVI

THE SHIP OF DEATH

SWEDE AND HELGA, from their hiding-place two miles inland, saw the *Miami* meet the Skraelings, and presently they saw the natives advancing single file up the path by which they themselves had ascended.

"I forgot to ask you," remarked Swede, "Can you shoot a—?" He fumbled for the Norse word.

"Rifle," she added in English.

"How do you know?" he asked, surprised.

"Why, that's what my Eric calls them," said she in Norse. "Yes, I can. He has had me practice with it empty, many times. But only twice or thrice with 'bullets' in it, for we are very short of 'ammunition.'"

"Well, now's your chance for some real practice," he announced, "for we have plenty of ammunition, and here come the Skraelings."

"Let's lie low and keep very quiet, until they get close," she cautioned.

So they waited. On came the leader of the single-file line of savages. On he came until, within about fifty yards of them, he suddenly stopped, uttered some sort of guttural remark of surprise, and pointed in their direction.

"He says 'Look!'" translated Helga in a whisper. "He must see us. No, don't fire, for he is pointing above us, at something else."

Swede and Helga turned their heads, and followed the direction of the pointing finger of the Skraeling. To their horror, they saw a gigantic gray snake, with curious markings, as big around as a barrel, and fully fifty feet long, wriggling down the mountainside above them. His forked red tongue, large as an average snake of the outer world, quivered in and out of his half-open mouth, and his expressionless eyes were deadly cold.

To stay where they were would mean to be devoured by this serpent, whereas either to fire at the beast or to flee from it would mean to be immediately attacked by the Skraelings.

But the enemy were evidently as frightened of the snake as they. A hurried command was passed down the advancing line, and the savages precipitately left the bed of the stream and started southward, deployed like a line of skirmishers.

The two fugitives, for their part, lost no time in scrambling to the top of the north bank of the stream under cover of the bushes which lined it. There they paused, not daring to proceed further, but ready to flee into the open if the serpent should force them to.

But the snake, disregarding both them and the Skraelings, crawled leisurely down the ravine toward the sea.

"Looks as though they were planning to attack some one," said Swede, glancing back toward the skirmish-line of Skraelings, and avoiding all further mention of the big snake.

"I think they are searching for us," replied Helga.

The two watched and waited, until the thin strung-out line disappeared in the distance. They saw the *Miami* also go south again. Then they started sneaking diagonally across country in the opposite direction, until they struck the head of the bay, from which point they followed the shore northward as before.

"Nothing ahead of us now," exulted Swede, "until we strike Altoonah's main army falling back this way before the advance of your Vikings."

"Halt!" a voice hailed them in English. "Stick up your hands!"

ALTHOUGH Swede could see no one, it was evident that the speaker had him covered. It would be foolhardy to reach for his gat now. If the newcomer proved to be unarmed, or insufficiently armed, there would be plenty of time later to attempt gunplay. So up went Swede's hands.

"Put your hands up," he translated to the girl, "or some one is going to shoot you."

"Capture is worse than death," she replied contemptuously, and drew her automatic.

A figure in the much-bedraggled remains of a yachting costume, stepped from behind a bush in front of them, an automatic in his hand.

"Yimmy's ghost!" exclaimed Swede, in a horror-stricken voice.

"Shall I shoot him?" asked Helga.

"It wouldn't do any good," replied her escort, through chattering teeth, "for he's dead already. I killed him myself two or three days ago."

"Cut out the Svenska," interjected Scarface peremptorily. "Talk United States, or I'll drill you. I'm not afraid of the lady, for I can tell by the way she holds her gat that she hasn't thrown the safety catch. See!"

And, still keeping Swede covered, he stepped quickly over to Helga and relieved her of the firearm which she was frantically trying to discharge at him.

She promptly sank to the ground and began to sob.

Scarface then helped himself to Swede's gun and both rifles.

"Now you can lower your hands," announced he, "for you look tired. Sit down and tell me who the lady is, and what you are doing here, and where is the rest of your gang."

"You sure you ain't ban dead?" asked Swede incredulously.

"Listen, Swede—I ought to know, oughtn't I?"

"But ve shot you down in your glider and couldn't find you," Swede objected, still unwilling to trust the evidence of his senses.

One fundamental principle with Scarface Boston Jimmy was that he always retained control and direction of any dialogue in which he was engaged. So he ignored the question implied in the other's remark.

"Never mind how I got here," said he. "The fact is that here I am, and I have you covered; so it's you that's going to answer the questions, not I. Who is the lady? What are you doing here? And what has become of the rest of your gang?"

"Vell," replied Swede, still disconcerted, "her name ban Helga."

"Not Helga Uppri!" exclaimed Scarface.

Startled by the exclamation, the girl looked up.

"*Yah*, Helga Uppri," said she. "Helga Redmond."

"Ve ban run away from Nick," added Swede. "Ve ban hunting for her Vikings."

"And where is Nick Fratelli now?"

"Yoost gone sout'."

"And the *Miami?*"

"Yoost gone sout', too. Nick ban in her."

"Fair enough!" ejaculated Jimmy. "So you've turned Viking? Well, so have I. Shake on it."

They shook. But, with Scandinavian persistency, Swede returned to his earlier doubt. "You ban dead, Yimmy?"

"I DON'T blame you for thinking so," replied Scarface tolerantly. "You shot me down all right, but I wasn't hit, except one bullet which just barely nipped my side. Bled quite badly, but no real harm done. The other fellow was killed, and I couldn't control the plane, so it crashed. The plane caught me and carried me under, and stuck on the bottom. I guess I must have been stunned for a few moments.

"When I came to, I found that my head was inside the cockpit, which was upside down, and full of air. So I stayed there just as long as I could stand it, and then ducked out and came to the surface. The *Miami* was chugging away. I lay on my back with my nose just barely out of water until you were at a safe distance, then swam ashore and cut straight inland, meaning to turn northward after a while and circle the Skraeling army.

"But this land must be narrower than I thought, for I soon struck the sea on the other side, and have been following the coast northward ever since. I hid while a body of Skraelings passed me just a little while ago, bound north."

"Nort'?" exclaimed Swede interrupting. "No, sout'!"

"What do you mean, south?" demanded Scarface. "If this is the opposite coast from the one we landed on, then that direction must be north."

"But it ban same coast," replied Swede, grinning. "You ban all twisted, Yimmy."

"Well, I must be!" ejaculated Scarface. "I'll bet I wandered around in a circle and came back to the same sea I started from. So that direction is south. And the rest of Altoonah's army is fighting the Vikings somewhere north?"

"Yah."

"What became of Helga's boat and the Vikings who were with her?"

"Vikings all shot up vit machine gun. Ve took everyting out of the boat and left it," explained Swede.

During all this conversation, Helga had been studying the handsome, though scarred, face of the young gangster. Now she held out one hand to him with a gracious gesture.

Jimmy, not knowing just what was expected of him, dropped on one knee, took the hand in one of his, and kissed it. Whether or not it was what was expected, the action seemed to please the girl, for she smiled.

"Here are your guns," said Scarface. "Come on, let's trek north, and try to get through the Skraeling lines and join the Vikings."

"Boat!" exclaimed Helga, pointing out to sea.

Both men followed the direction of her finger. Far out at sea was a dragon-prowed ship, with sail furled, being propelled southward by lusty rowers, against a light head wind.

"The fools!" exclaimed Scarface Jimmy. "They can't stand up for a minute against a machine gun. We must head them off. Come on!"

WHEN Jimmy had failed to return to the plateau city, Angus Selkirk dispatched another glider, and not waiting for its report, at once set out down the Skraeling trail, with all the remaining available warriors of the plateau, leaving Nils Uppri, much against his will, in charge. Nils might be bishop, and hence the nominal ruler of all this realm, but his extreme youthfulness compelled him to defer to the judgment of his elders, even though he outranked them.

However, as soon as Angus had left, Nils asserted himself, and evolved what seemed to him, deprived of the advice of the one local man who understood Chicago gangsters and American firearms, to be a first-rate plan, namely, to sail south in a trading ship which had just arrived, and engage single-handed in a naval battle with the *Miami*.

He could not conceive how a handful of these outlandish Americans, on whatever kind of a boat, with whatever kind of weapons, could be any match at all for one of the superb dragon ships of the Norsemen.

The Norse ship was fully manned, so the shortage of warriors on the plateau would not hamper him in his undertaking. There were plenty of old graybeards to assume the duties of government in the city which he was leaving. So he donned his armor, turned over the reins of government, and made for the beach. Several of the women and old men came down with him, to see him off.

Thus it was that his sister Astrid, his beautiful cousin Borghild, and the little Portuguese minx Theresa, were all on the beach when the final preparations were being made for sailing.

Not a word of Norse did little Terry understand, but when Borghild pointed south and said, "Yimmy. *Boat. Komm!*" she caught the idea, and nodded.

The group on the beach watched the stalwart craft row out to sea and turn southward. Bishop Nils Uppri, from the stern beside the helmsman, waved a proud farewell. His people waved back and cheered, for they loved the brave boy.

Then Astrid turned, to look for Borghild and Theresa, but they were nowhere to be seen; inquiry of all those who had been on the beach produced no information, nor even any clews.

Meanwhile the Viking ship rowed south with furled sail, the crew taking turns at rowing and sleeping.

It was not until eight or ten hours later that one of the men, in disturbing one of the sleeping-mats, disturbed also Theresa and Borghild, whom the mat had served to conceal. The two were at once haled before the bishop, who gave them a quite unecclesiastical dressing-down.

But he was not as effective as he might have been. In the first place, he was too young. In the second place, Borghild was his cousin, who had grown up with him from childhood. And, in the third place, little Terry couldn't understand a word of his tirade.

"Gee, Your Reverence," said she, grinning, "that don't mean nothing in my young life. You'll have to speak United States, to get by with me. *Yee forstaar ikka.*"

Which was all the Norse she knew.

NILS DIDN'T dare turn back, for fear that Angus might have returned to the plateau, and might put a stop to his venture. Nils, as boy bishop, presented somewhat the same pitiable figure as King George of England, begging his prime minister for permission to pardon Lord Mayor McSwiney, and being refused—perhaps the most pathetic occurrence in all the history of the outer world.

Accordingly there was nothing for Nils to do but put up with the presence of the two girls. Terry's presence, at least, did not

particularly irk him. But he couldn't discriminate, before all
these men, between her and his cousin.

In due course of time, the dragon ship of Nils Uppri passed
the spot where the Viking army was slowly driving south the
main body of the Skraelings; but Nils did not stop, or even draw
near to the shore, for fear that older and wiser heads among
the Norse warriors might attempt to dissuade him from his
undertaking. And thus it was that eventually his barge hove in
sight of Scarface, Swede and Helga, as already related.

The attempt of these three to head him off proved unavailing.
They stood on the promontory and waved and waved and
shouted, but the Viking barge swept on to the southward, the
lusty song of the rowers drowning the warning voices.

The *Miami* was still in sight not far away, as it had slowed
its engines to keep pace with the searching skirmish-line of
savages. Presently the watchers on shore saw the *Miami* sight
the Norse ship, turn around, and advance to meet it. They held
their breaths with horror at the impending calamity.

Bravely the dragon ship steered straight at the *Miami*, to
ram and sink it, the rowers speeding up to their fastest stroke.
But expert as were these navigators out of the past, they were
no match, in maneuvering, for a motor yacht, undermanned
though it was.

So the *Miami* blithely side-stepped the charge; and, almost
before the Vikings realized what was up, circled their ship with
the deadly machine gun turned loose. In less than one ammu-
nition-belt, it was all over. The once-proud Norse craft was
drifting leaderless upon the sea. Nils Uppri had been one of
the first to fall, and not another Viking stood alive on the dragon
ship.

The watchers on the shore saw the *Miami* tie up alongside
the barge for a few minutes, and then cut loose and chug south
again to rejoin the Skraelings. For Nick had made but a cursory
search of the conquered boat, merely long enough to slit the
throats of any wounded who showed signs of life, and to rob

the dead of their jewelry and more ornate weapons and clothing. Of provisions he had no need, as he was fully stocked from the loot of Helga's ship. And he was not to be diverted, except temporarily, from his vengeful search for Swede and Helga.

Swede's defection had hampered him considerably, but he had stationed Cicero and Friday at the machine gun, and Charley Loy at the engines. The Chink might not know anything about machinery, but he could shift gears in response to bell-signals from the pilot-house, and could realize full well that any monkeying with the engines would mean his instant demise.

As the *Miami* proceeded south once more, the spoils of war were divided, and soon every one on board, even including Charley Loy, was busy accoutering himself in Norse clothing and armament. This preoccupation accounted for their not being quite as alert as they should have been, during the important events which immediately followed.

A SLIGHT shift in the wind slowly drifted the dragon ship shoreward.

"Let's meet her, when she beaches," suggested Helga, through Swede as an interpreter. "There may still be some alive on board, who may need our aid."

Jimmy assented, and so the three walked slowly along, still keeping under cover of the bushes, until they came to the spot toward which the boat was being borne by the rapidly freshening wind.

When it finally bumped upon the shallows, the three waded furtively out and climbed on board.

The mutilated and stripped bodies were a sad sight even to the two hardened Chicago gangsters. But to Helga they were more. Many of them were old friends and acquaintances. All were quite, quite dead, thanks either to American machine gun bullets, or to the frightful efficiency of the throat-slashing savages.

Under directions from the saddened princess, the two men carried the bodies, one by one, to the stern and covered each with a sleeping-mat.

The sight sobered Scarface Boston Jimmy, as the realization swept over him that *this was exactly what he himself had planned to do.* If it had not been for the defection of his chief lieutenant, Nick the Rat, this crime might now be on his own head. The real change in Scarface Boston Jimmy, and the definite abandonment of his dreams of empire, dated from that moment— and was strengthened by his relief and joy when Theresa and Borghild, unscathed, were found cowering beneath the pile of sleeping-mats. It was a heart-warming sight, that reunion of old friends.

Borghild flung herself upon Scarface, and clung to him, sobbing, "Yimmy, Yimmy."

Helga raised her eyebrows for a moment, and then smiled, tolerantly. Then, because of Borghild's preoccupation, Swede introduced Terry to Helga.

But suddenly Borghild broke away with a cry, "Nils, Nils, my cousin Nils. Where is he?"

"Nils? Was he on board?" exclaimed Helga and Scarface simultaneously, though in different languages.

"Sure," and *"Yah,"* replied Terry and Borghild.

And immediately there began a frantic search among such corpses as had not yet been moved. The body of the boy bishop was soon discovered, lying in the bow where he had stood, with a party of boarders, directing the attack. The three women flung themselves upon it in tears.

But Scarface shouted, "Lay off it! He may still be alive."

ELBOWING the frantic women one side, he examined the body. The throat had not been slit. No wounds noticeable any- where except one in the temple which smeared the face with blood.

Lifting the shirt of chain-mail, the gangster applied his ear to the chest.

"He's not dead!" he shouted. "Water! Quick!"

Theresa brought some at once in one of the cooking utensils and dashed it in Nils's face, and soon the blue eyes of the young Viking opened, stared vaguely around, rested on the girl bending over him, and paused there.

"Where am I?" Nils groaned.

"We must get him ashore at once to safety," asserted Scarface.

But, while they had been at work, the wind had made a complete about-turn, and they were now a hundred yards or more at sea and being rapidly blown further.

"Let's get up the sail and tack back," suggested Jimmy. "Hey, Swede, ask Mrs. Redmond and Miss Hoglund if they know how to hoist it, and then you help them. Miss Ferreira, you stay with the bishop. I'll clear away the broken oars, and then steer. Hurry!"

It was a rash and mistaken move. The Viking ship, in its apparently unmanned condition, might have drifted out to sea unnoticed: but the moment the gaudily striped sail began to rise, their maneuver was instantly sighted by the distant *Miami*, which at once put about, and came after them, full speed.

No time now to tack.

"We've got to run for it, before the wind," announced Scarface, grabbing the steering oar.

Soon the sail was fully flung to the offshore breeze, and Swede and the two Viking girls finished clearing away the oars, while Scarface steered, and Theresa soothed and tended Nils.

The wind grew steadily stronger and swung to the northward. Its strengthening brought the speed of the dragon ship almost up to that of the craft which was seeking to overhaul it. But the shift of wind to the northward enabled the *Miami* to follow in a smaller circle, and thus to overtake it with great rapidity.

As the *Miami* came within rifle range, those aboard the Viking barge could see Cicero and Friday busily getting the bow machine gun ready for action. In a few minutes its deadly spray would be spattering upon the fleeing vessel.

CHAPTER XVII

INTO UNKNOWN SEAS

"GET BELOW!" SHOUTED Scarface, as the rattle of the *Miami's* machine gun started, and the leaden hail began splashing about the stern of his fleeing Viking ship. "I'll steer until they get me, damn them, then Swede can take the oar—one by one, as long as there are any of us left."

"And not fight back, chief?" exclaimed Swede in surprise.

Helga said something in Norse to her girl cousin, and then to Swede.

"She says," translated the latter, "that Borghild and she can take turns at steering, so we two men can use the rifles."

"Fair enough!" agreed Scarface. "Let's go!"

And soon Borghild Hoglund was clinging to the long oar which passed through the ring in the stern, while Helga and the two gangsters were lying on the deck beside her, the men discharging clip after clip at the oncoming *Miami*. It must have taken considerable courage for Borghild to expose herself thus, while her companions lay in comparative safety; but it was necessary; and she was a Viking.

The stream of bullets from the machine gun found the stern of the barge, and rose slowly toward its four occupants. Borghild shrank involuntarily at her oar, but the two riflemen kept coolly at their work. Although their Springfields slightly outranged the .30-caliber machine bow gun, yet Cicero and Friday had the advantage of being able to play their weapon like a hose.

Once let them get completely within range, and the annihilation of the fugitives would be sudden and complete.

A stray soaring shot nicked Borghild, and she toppled. Disregarding the pursuing bullets, Jimmy sprang to his feet and caught the falling body in his arms, while Helga manned the oar, and Swede kept up his fire.

The rattle of the machine gun stopped, as Friday dropped, wounded, to the deck of the *Miami*. But Altoonah took the wheel, and Nick Fratelli, in person, stepped on deck to assist Cicero with the deadly weapon.

"Get him, Swede! Get the Rat!" urged Scarface, as he lowered Borghild to the deck and frantically searched for her wound.

Tat-tat-tat-tat! began the machine gun—then stopped abruptly, as Cicero Tony clapped his hand to his chest and staggered backward, falling in a heap on the *Miami's* deck.

"I tank I vinged his sore shoulder," grinned Swede.

But it was soon evident that Cicero was merely incapacitated as a machine gunner, rather than put out of business. Fratelli assisted him into the pilot-house, and then emerged with Altoonah (crutches and all), whom he seemed to be frantically instructing how to feed the piece.

At this moment Borghild came to her senses. She had been shot through the calf of one leg, and had merely fainted. Helga peremptorily sent her below to relieve Terry in caring for Nils. When Terry came on deck, Helga dropped prone on the deck and picked up the rifle which Scarface had been using.

Tat-tat-tat! went the machine gun again.

Crack! spoke Helga's rifle.

Swede and Altoonah rolled on their respective decks, each clutching at his throat.

"Dey got me, I tank," groaned Johnson hoarsely, then coughed up some blood.

Helga dropped her rifle, and took the wounded man's head in her lap. He smiled at her and patted one of her arms with his hand.

"Lady," said he, "I tank I vorship you."

Then a paroxysm of bloody coughing ensued, his body stiffened, then went limp.

The Norse princess lowered his head softly to the deck; and, with fire in her eye, picked up her rifle again.

"Viking!" she announced proudly.

NICK FRATELLI had disappeared. Scarface and Helga kept up a steady fire on the windows of the pilot-house of the *Miami*, but that craft continued to overhaul them. In spite of the fact that Scarface now had two available riflemen to the *Miami's* one, yet if the *Miami* once got alongside, its squad of Skraelings could undoubtedly board them and overpower them by sheer weight of numbers; and this quite evidently was Nick Fratelli's plan.

With Swede Johnson dead, further communication between the Americans and the Vikings on board the Norse ship was rendered impossible.

"I'm going up in the bow," explained Scarface to Terry, "so as to prevent their landing there."

Then he left. Helga started to follow him, but he motioned her back. She flashed him a look of supreme contempt. Leaving two women to protect him, was he, while he took to cover? But when the *Miami* ranged alongside, and he opened fire from his new position, she understood, and was ashamed of having doubted him.

The *Miami* was now directly opposite them on the port side, and began slowly to draw in closer. Yet still not a head showed anywhere, for fear of Jimmy's and Helga's marksmanship.

Scarface caught sight of Nick's face in a mirror hanging in the pilot-house of the *Miami*, and instantly shattered the glass with a bullet. Fratelli had quite evidently been using that mirror to steer by, and his task would from now on be rendered more difficult.

How could he resusitate her on that wave-drenched rock?

And then a new and unmistakable note was heard in the chugging of the *Miami's* motors. Jimmy cocked his ears, and then nearly laughed aloud.

"Keep it up, Terry," he shouted. "They're out of gas!"

Terry nodded, and clutched her oar tighter. But Fratelli also suddenly realized the situation, and swinging his helm sharply, attempted to bear directly down on them. It looked as though he were going to make it, although his engines were now coughing and missing. The engines stopped, but the *Miami* had sufficient steerage-way to carry her bow squarely into the stern of the dragon ship, unless something happened to prevent.

Shooting a whole clip into the windows of the pilot-house, Scarface reloaded and hurried aft; while on board the *Miami*, the Skraelings surged on deck and opened fire—quite aimlessly, however.

"Starboard your helm!" shouted Scarface.

"How?" shouted back bewildered little Terry.

"That way! Push your oar that way! Hard!"

Theresa obeyed, with every ounce of strength that was in her, and the stern of the Norse ship swung suddenly to port out of the path of the oncoming *Miami*, just in time.

As the *Miami* swept by under their stern, Scarface arrived on the run beside Terry and Helga.

"Straighten her up again," he shouted, but Terry needed no command, for the steering-oar swung around of its own accord in hands too tired to prevent, and the ship under the influence of the wind automatically resumed its earlier course. Scarface dropped on one knee and let the Skraelings have a full clip, whereupon they broke and crowded back into the cabin of the *Miami*.

"We've won!" Scarface shouted. "Licked 'em to a frazzle!"

But Terry interrupted with, "Gee, Mr. Jimmy, look!"

He looked. The *Miami* had swung around again, so that its bow was pointing toward them, and its inertia was still carrying it in their wake. Nick Fratelli and Cicero Tony Schultz were at the machine gun, and still well within range.

"Duck!" shouted Scarface, grabbing both girls and dragging them with him into the hold, just as the gun let loose.

THE BULLETS pattered on the stern, and tore through the planking, but those in the hold of the Viking barge piled up sleeping mats and crawled behind them before any harm had been done.

"A narrow escape!" breathed Scarface Jimmy. "Now all we've got to do is lie low until the wind pulls us away from them. But, if we had only seen those two before they got to the gun, it would have been a different story. Too bad!"

Presently the patter of the bullets ceased, and then the *tat-tat-tat!* of the machine gun itself ceased too. They were out of range at last, and Nick the Rat knew it.

The young Nils was feeling much better. Although he had chafed at being out of the fight, his cockiness had been completely destroyed by the fatal outcome of his venture; and so, being weaponless, he had made no attempt to come on deck during the recent battle. Helga dressed Borghild's wound, and then she and the two Americans laid out all the remaining bodies, including poor Swede's.

As they were completing this sad task, Theresa remarked, "It must be nearly night; see how dark it's getting."

But it was not the darkness of night, for night never comes within the earth. Instead, it was an impending storm. Drops of rain began to fall, and they could hear the wind howling overhead, as it swept by in the higher strata at even a faster rate than it was blowing on the surface of the sea.

"*Komm!*" ordered Helga, as she led them forward to the mast, and indicated that the sail must be lowered at once.

But not clear down, for they must have steerage-way, to keep them heading with the wind, and thus avoid getting broadside to the waves, and foundering. Accordingly they furled the gaudily striped sail down to the lowest reef.

Meanwhile the day grew blacker and blacker, the nearest thing to actual night which the Americans had seen since entering the interior of the earth. The wind was now from the north; rain fell in slanting torrents, while the Viking barge scudded along before the fury of the blast, with the Norse bishop, the two Norse women, little Terry, and Scarface Boston Jimmy taking turns, two by two at the steering-oar. They spoke little during that storm, partly because Fate, in removing Swede Johnson, had removed the only bridge which spanned the linguistic gulf between the three Vikings and the two Americans, but mostly because they were too busy and because the roar of the wind and the rain drowned out their voices.

HOW LONG the storm continued will never be known. Shift after shift, they all labored to hold the ship with the veering wind. Drenched, chilled, exhausted, they labored on. It all seemed like a nightmare, an unending treadmill. Of the five, the three Vikings stood it the best, for they were used to timeless time.

When it became evident that the storm was to continue indefinitely, they reluctantly heaved all the bodies overboard, Bishop Nils reciting the liturgy for death at sea. And, after all, what burial could be more fitting for these brave seafarers than to be sent to the bottom of the ocean amid wind and driving rain?

While, two by two, they clung to the straining stern-oar, the members of the party who were temporarily off duty, ate, or tried to dry themselves, or dozed fitfully. As shift dragged after shift, they devoted more time to dozing, until finally everything degenerated into a weary round of steering, dropping exhausted to the deck, stupor, and being awakened to steer again.

The one and only redeeming feature was that there is nothing better for wounds than rain. Ask the men who have been left outside of emergency-dressing stations in France, so hopelessly wounded that men with lesser injuries, men whom there was hope of saving, were treated first. Yet some of those who were given up have been miraculously kept alive, their wounds dressed by a timely downpour. They know!

At last the five voyagers completely lost awareness of events.

Presumably they continued their cycle of duty as in a trance, but this can never be known. Scarface afterward remembered the round of steering and sleeping; then came an absolute blank. And then—

Swimming in the angry surges!

He did not even remember the boat crashing. Merely that he woke up to find himself struggling in the surf. And still the black, black night of storm.

A wave hurled Scarface against a rock, stunning him. But he managed to crawl upon the rock and hold on. It was small, scarcely five feet across, and every wave washed over it; but it was rough, and so afforded a handhold and a foothold.

Then the darkness grew lighter. The rain ceased, although the wind still drove on. Looking back into the teeth of the gale,

Scarface saw a woman's body floating directly toward his rock, with her golden hair spread out like seaweed awash.

In an instant, he had plunged into the water to windward, to intercept the body and prevent its dashing against the rock. As he staggered back, beaten by the waves, with the body in his arms, he saw that it was Borghild.

There was no sign anywhere of Nils, Helga, or Terry.

A few splintered boards, floating by, were the only relics of the Viking ship.

CHAPTER XVIII

BACK IN THE COAL AGE

THE RAIN HAD completely ceased. The wind was dying down. But the surges of the angry sea continued to break over Scarface's standing-place.

The body he clasped was that of his beloved Borghild. Was she dead? And, if not, how could he administer first aid on that wave-washed rock?

Shaking the water out of his black beard, he glanced around him in despair. To the leeward, through the mist and spray, he finally made out a spit of sand not wholly covered by the waves. It was her only chance for life!

So he plunged into the surf with his precious burden and tried to swim. He was rapidly carried, more by the waves than by his own exertions, toward that bit of land. He reached it. He stumbled to his feet, only to be immediately beaten down again. He staggered inland, with her body thrown across one of his broad shoulders, her arms and head and golden tresses hanging down behind, one of his arms hooked across her knees, his other arm fending before him. Thus he made the shore.

There was no barrel to roll the body on, but he reflected that the jouncing which it had received upon his shoulder going through the surf had probably been sufficient to discharge all the water from the lungs.

So, quickly laying Borghild face down upon the sand, he turned her head on one side resting on her arm, forced open her mouth, and gave a pull at her tongue to clear her air passages. Then he knelt astride her legs, placed both his hands, with fingers widespread, about her short-ribs, and commenced a slow rhythmic pressure and release.

All this he did with machine-like precision, as though the saving of lives from drowning was an everyday routine affair with him. And yet his mind seemed strangely detached from the whole performance. While his indomitable will was driving his body to perform these acts, his mind was saying over and over again: "I love her. I love her. Oh, God—have pity on me— help me to save her! Give her back to me."

As a matter of fact, this was the first time that Scarface Boston Jimmy had ever tried to resuscitate any one. He had not even ever practiced it. But in his avid reading, and his insatiable search for knowledge, he had salted away the needful information, and now he remembered it with surprising accuracy.

After a while he became calmer, and began to consider the situation, as he toiled.

"The books said," he ruminated, "that people have been brought to, after even three-quarters of an hour of this."

He looked instinctively at his wrist-watch, which was still running, in spite of this, its second immersion. Then he set his jaws.

"I shall not stop until I drop! Oh, my Borghild, come back to me!"

The artificial respiration continued. An ordinarily strong man ought to be able to keep this up almost indefinitely, but Jimmy had been steering the Viking ship day after day through the storm, until he had become unconscious with the strain, and then had been forced to swim for his life. He was water-logged and weak. The rhythmic motion would not keep up, as it should, by mere virtue of its own rhythm; it required the constant attention of his mind and will.

BUT HIS hands were becoming numb. He could no longer feel the cold girlish form beneath his outstretched fingers. Excruciating pain shot from his elbows to his shoulders and across his back, until the numbness, creeping up his arms, began to deaden the pain. The back of his head ached dully. It was difficult to keep his eyes open. His breathing became dry and choked.

He wanted—oh, so much—to collapse beside the body of his Borghild, and sleep there forever. Time and again he shook himself awake, on the verge of dozing.

He could no longer control his fingers, and suddenly he realized that he was kneading merely with his wrists, with the ends of the bones of his lower arms. It was as though his hands had gone.

This realization horrified him and brought him to his senses for a moment. Then the numbness reached his elbow-joints, and he could no longer push at all.

Shocked, despairing, but undaunted, he leaned forward to take up the forlorn task with his elbows against her ribs; but the attempt threw him off his balance, and he fell forward prone on the sand, beside the body of the girl he loved.

He struggled to rise, but could not, and so lay still. His head swam, his senses reeled, his eyes clouded. Through the mist, he could hear an angel-voice calling:

"Yimmy! Yimmy!"

It was Borghild, welcoming him to heaven. Then he knew no more.

The next thing that he realized was that he was suddenly and completely awake. He was lying on his side in the sand. The pale, quiet face of the Viking maiden was within a few inches of his own.

The blue eyes opened, and the lips smiled a little wan smile.

"Yimmy," she breathed.

With a superhuman effort, he craned his neck forward and kissed the blue lips, whereat a slight flush mantled her white cheek. Then his head fell back again upon the sand.

After a time, he opened his eyes again, and looked at her, but he had no energy for any further bodily movement than this. Her eyes were closed now, but her chest was regularly rising and falling. As he gazed, however, she sighed deeply and stopped breathing.

The sight galvanized Jimmy to action. Dragging himself to his knees, he tried to wrap his nerveless arms about her. Failing this, he leaned over, caught himself with one shoulder against the sand, and covered her pale face with kisses.

Another deep sigh, and her regular breathing began again. Her eyes opened, and again she blushed.

"That'll bring the blood back to your cheeks!" exclaimed Jimmy, joyously, as he struggled to his feet.

With a supreme effort, he lifted his arms aloft and threw every ounce of his will into an attempt at wiggling his fingers.

Slowly the fingers began to move. Pins and needles shot from his shoulders to his finger-tips, as the circulation painfully resumed its course. Gradually the control of his muscles returned.

After one last spreading and stretching of every finger to its utmost, he stooped and gathered Borghild in his arms. She was still alive but very weak. It was imperative to get her somewhere at once, where she could have warmth and dry clothes and rest. Hot-water bottles for the soles of her feet, dry blankets over her, warm bouillon to drink, and all that sort of thing.

The gangster bent over and kissed her again, then looked around. The sun was still clouded. The wind had died down to a gentle breeze, but great rollers still burst upon the beach and dashed the spray across the spit of sand on which he stood.

Far off, a mile or so away, the sandbar joined at right angles a tree-clad mainland, a vast continent evidently, which curved ever upward in the distance, until it merged with the heavens above. Toward this mainland Scarface set resolutely forth with his limp burden. But the sand was soft and shifting, and many times he was forced to lay her down and rest, ere he reached his goal.

As he neared the woods, they did not appear as inviting as they had from the distance, for they were unlike any woods which he had ever seen before. Huge ferns as tall as elms. Palm trees even taller. Between the trees rose club-moss and lichens almost as tall as the ferns, forming an impenetrable-appearing thicket.

SCARFACE felt suddenly dwarfed, like Alice in Wonderland. Even the sand at his feet bore out the illusion, for it was large and pebbly, and strewn with periwinkle-shaped shells the size of a man's head. Along the edge of the wood flew dragon-flies as large as eagles. Scarface began to wonder if he and his fair companion hadn't perhaps shrunk to midgets, after all.

The beach by the edge of the wood was high and untouched by the spray. The central sun shone hotly down. So Scarface laid Borghild tenderly on the sand, and removed her wet clothing as far as was decent. Then stripping some palm-fronds, he improvised a clothes rack and wrung out the wet garments and hung them to dry.

Borghild lay listlessly and watched him. When the wash had all been put out, he felt of the girl's hands and feet. Icy cold, in spite of the tropic warmth. Tenderly he chafed them, until she too began to recover her normal temperature. Not until then did he make an attempt to dry some of his own clothes.

Then languid and peaceful—for the pangs of hunger had not yet begun to assail them—the two lay side by side on the sand in the warmth of the life-giving central sun. They had each other, which was something, in their grief for their lost companions. They drifted weakly off to sleep, without realizing that they were doing so.

They awoke æons later, rested and ravenous.

What awakened them was a clattering of the pebbles, as though an army were on the march. The wind had completely died. The sea rocked almost imperceptibly with an oily swell.

And up the beach from the sea, there advanced a far-flung skirmish-line of fish! Fish the size of horses, walking—actually walking, on pectoral and anal fins, like four legs—walking toward them from the sea, like some horrible cavalry of Neptune's lower depths.

The mouths of these fish were large, wide-open, as if grinning, lined with a serrated row of shark-like teeth.

Every once in a while, when two of this advancing horde would get too close to each other and bump together, they would snap viciously at each other, and then move apart again.

"This is no place for us!" exclaimed Scarface, leaping to his feet. "Come on!"

Stiffly the girl sprang up, and stood beside him.

"*Komm!*" said she, and held out her hand.

Together they raced up the beach to the very edge of the wood, looking for a place to enter. Meanwhile the menacing line of amphibious fish continued their relentless advance. A transition form, perhaps, of prehistoric life emerging from the sea to begin their own evolution into frog, reptile, bird, mammal, man, and even beyond.

Finally the two found a place where they could penetrate the protecting forest a little way. There they stopped, to see how far the fish would advance. But the fish did not come all the way. Instead, they lay down on the pebbles and basked in the sun.

"If they aren't going to eat us," remarked the man, "let's eat one of them."

So saying, he tore an extra-large frond from one of the palms, stripped off its leaves, and strode forth from his hiding place. The fish nearest him reared up on its front fins, standing almost as high as he did, and growled. Jimmy promptly whacked it across the snout with his stick, whereat it charged him.

He retreated slowly, belaboring the creature as he fell back. Several other fish near by, disturbed by the commotion, got clumsily to their feet and stared stupidly around. Jimmy thought of using his revolver, but decided not to waste any ammunition, unless absolutely necessary.

The front fins of the attacking fish gave way just as it reached the edge of the wood; and Jimmy, quick to sense his advantage, beat the beast violently about the head, until it lay panting on the ground.

Borghild, from within the wood, clapped her little hands with glee. She didn't know what the fight was all about; but, being a true Viking maid, she enjoyed a fight for the fight's sake.

HAVING got the huge fish at his mercy, Jimmy stepped into close quarters, drew his hunting-knife, and slit the huge creature's throat, so that the fierce head rolled severed on the ground.

Here was food, food in abundance. But for whom? Even as he arose from his gory job, the fish pack with roars and growls rushed forward, driving Jimmy back to the cover of the woods. Hungrily the cannibal amphibians fell upon their deceased brother, and tore the body to pieces. All that trouble for nothing!

Borghild, not realizing the loss, was still applauding.

This would never do! There must be some way to get a victim and keep it from being devoured. Wait: he had it! Build a fire! Fire for two purposes—to cook one fish, and to keep the other fish away. It was worth trying.

So he waited until the ravenous pack of tiger-like creatures had gorged themselves—including eating several of their number who had been slain fighting over the feast—and had returned to their nap.

Without disturbing their slumbers, he stepped cautiously out of his hiding-place and, motioning Borghild to accompany and assist him, he began gathering driftwood which lay along the high-water line near the top of the beach. The fish occasionally growled or grunted as they came too near, but did not interfere with them.

When quite a sizable pile of wood had been collected, Jimmy shredded a few sticks for kindlings, and pulled out his patent cigar-lighter. But of course the thing wouldn't work, for it was sopping wet; Jimmy sadly realized that it would never work again, for the alcohol would evaporate before the water.

What did people do under such circumstances? They twiddled sticks, didn't they? He was prepared to try this as a last resort, but wasn't there some simpler way? Eric had used a burning glass, in the story, he remembered. Too bad he hadn't one.

A watch seems to be the involuntary answer to most questions. Ask a man the day of the week, or the latest quotation of General Motors, and he will—like as not—glance automatically at his watch, before answering you. In his perplexity, Scarface glanced at his watch, and it gave him the answer!

Instantly he smiled, whipped out his knife, and pried off the crystal. But unfortunately the lens wasn't thick enough to focus the sunlight into a spot sufficiently small for his purpose.

Borghild had been watching him with interest and understanding. Now she offered a suggestion.

"Yarl Angus," she began, followed by an utterly unintelligible string of Norse words.

Her companion shook his head.

"*Yee forstaar ikka,*" said he, grinning. It was his one Norse accomplishment—admitting he didn't understand.

So she snatched the watch-crystal from his hand, and made a motion as though pouring something into it. He caught on at once. Of course.

"Add water and serve," said he.

So, taking back the little piece of glass, he rushed suddenly between the dozing fish, down to the sea, where he filled his lens with water. But getting back wasn't so easy. He couldn't rush back through the pack without spilling the precious fluid, so he tried tiptoeing cautiously between them. But one of them, disturbed, snapped at his leg, and he jumped and spilled the water. He had to cut and run for the sheltering woods.

But again Borghild was helpful. This time she indicated his knife. When he gave it to her, she stripped a piece of bark from one of the trees, and with it she fashioned a rude cup. This would enable him to rush between the finny sleepers without spilling too much water.

"Say, you're a regular pal," he exclaimed.

The words meant nothing to her, but she understood the tone of voice, and so smiled.

"I've half a mind to kiss you for that," he continued.

So he did, and got his face slapped. They were getting on splendidly. The slap seemed to wipe out the affront effectively. She smiled again and handed him the cup. Once more he ventured down to the sea.

THIS time he got the water safely through. But before he lit the fire, he fashioned a second club, so that Borghild could help him "get" their dinner. For he noticed that the fish were beginning to become restless, which foreboded plenty of trouble.

The fire started readily enough in the shavings which he had made, but it required considerable care and coaxing from the two of them before it finally developed into a real blaze, for the surfaces of all the sticks and logs were soaking wet from the recent storm.

At last, however, the two of them arose from their preoccupying task well satisfied, and dusted off their hands and knees, preparatory to slaughtering their meal. Then they looked around for a likely victim.

Not until then did they notice a crunching of pebbles of which they had been only dimly conscious during all their fire-making. The fish were marching seaward again. Their dinner was leaving them!

With a howl of dismay, the two rushed down the beach, brandishing their clubs—to reach the edge just as the last amphibian slid clumsily into the ocean and mockingly disappeared from sight.

"Hell!" ejaculated Jimmy.

Borghild caught the tone, and uttered emphatically some equally questionable word in Norse. Then the two looked at each other and grinned. After the many hard knocks that Fate had handed them, the addition of one more was almost funny.

But the humor of the situation did not do away with its grimness. No food; no fresh water; nothing to do but sit down, wait, and take turns at watching until the walking fish should return for their next sun-bath.

But the question was: how often did these beasts come out to bask? It might be hourly, or it might be once in a lifetime.

Nor would the return of the fish provide any drinking water!

If they waited where they were, their food might come back to them, it is true, but they were in immediate need of fresh water. The absence of the carnivorous walking fish, while it deprived them of food, yet also permitted them the freedom of the beach. The obvious thing to do was to walk along the beach in search of a spring or brook. And, while they were about it, they might just as well walk northward, for that way lay home, though how many hundreds or thousands of miles away, the storm-tossed pair knew not.

So, gathering up the rest of their garments, they started out.

THE SUN was hot, and they were tired, and weak, and hungry, and thirsty. Very hungry, and oh so thirsty!

They came at last to a ledge of rocks projecting into the sea. In hollows of the rocks were pools of rain-water, now rapidly drying, and hence very stale. But it was water, real water, and they drank deeply of it, and were much refreshed.

In salt pools further out, they found giant sea-snails alive. So another fire was built, up by the edge of the woods. There was no danger of setting these lush woods on fire, and no harm done even if they did so.

When the fire was fairly started, Scarface leaned against a tree for a moment. Instantly he found himself in the midst of a display of fireworks such as he had never observed in Chicago either on the Fourth of July or on a ward picnic. The air around him was completely filled with sparks, so that he could not see another thing.

As he vanished from sight in a shower of sparks, Borghild shrieked.

"Yimmy!" she called, and regardless of danger to herself, she rushed through the fireworks and flung her arms around his neck.

Her onslaught forced him back against the tree, and as he bumped it, another display of pyrotechnics ensued. Borghild shrieked again and clung to him all the tighter.

The sparks did not appear to have burned either of them; and Jimmy, always an opportunist, held the girl to him, and soothed and kissed her, without any remonstrance on her part. Whatever caused the fireworks, he liked the effect.

At last, somewhat calmed and reassured, she started to draw away, bashfully and a bit reproachfully. Whereat Jimmy had an idea.

The tree behind him appeared to be the cause of the fiery phenomenon, so he kicked it violently, and was rewarded by another shower of sparks, which sent Borghild once more into his arms.

But unfortunately Borghild soon caught on, and drew away from him, with an expression which said as plainly as words, "You're doing this on purpose, you know you are."

"Of course I am," said Jimmy aloud, and grinned his disarming grin.

The girl smiled, walked demurely back, and kissed him shyly, virginally, only to be immediately seized in his arms again and devoured, this time without either excuse or resistance. She was his, all his, from then on.

It may be possible to live on "bread and cheese and kisses," but the bread and the cheese form an indispensable part of such a diet. So the two placed some of the huge sea-snails, shell and all, on the coals of the fire, and smothered them in seaweed to roast. The result, to their relief, proved delectable.

After the meal, the two sat hand in hand for a while, just gazing out to sea. The water, lapping at the rocks, made a pleasing sound. The rocks and the sea and the beach, a pleasing sight. Peace at last, and love, after all that they had gone through.

AFTER a while, Jimmy got up. "Want some more fireworks?" he asked, and shook the tree.

Again a shower of sparks. The girl clapped her hands with glee.

The tree was a gigantic club-moss. Of course! Lycopodium. Jimmy remembered having read of the use of lycopodium powder in the manufacture of old-fashioned fireworks, and how boys would often gather club-moss in the woods and shake it over candle-flames. Well, here was lycopodium powder by the ton!

Walking along the beach a little way from the fire, he spread out beneath a lycopodium tree one of Borghild's voluminous garments, which he had been carrying, and then shook down about a bushel of the brown grains. These he carted back to near the fire, and he and the girl amused themselves for quite a while by tossing handfuls into the fire and watching the results.

A fish jumped just beyond the ledge of rock. That gave Scarface an idea. So he bent a pin taken from one of Borghild's clasps, fastened it to a cord from one of her garments, baited it with a piece of sea-snail, and with care and patience, caught a fish for supper.

They stayed by the rocky ledge, fishing, cooking, eating and taking turns at watching and sleeping, until the fresh water in the rock-pools dried up. At last they determined to start north again.

They had gone only a short distance when they stopped, horrified; the way was blocked by a gigantic long-necked toad, about the size of a giraffe, hopping toward them down the beach.

Instantly they rushed to the fire and replenished it, relying on the traditional fear of animals for fire. But this prehistoric toad quite evidently had never heard of the tradition. He hopped leisurely up to the fire, and blinked at them first with one eye and then with the other.

Scarface put a protecting arm around the girl and drew her back. The beast reached one paw out and tentatively touched the blaze, then hastily snatched it back and shook it in a puzzled sort of way. Finally it reached its neck across the flames toward the pair.

It was evident that if the idea should penetrate the creature's thick skull to hop around the fire, they would be driven away from their only protection. Jimmy was just about to draw his revolver, when a better idea occurred to him. Beside them lay a pile of the lycopodium powder with which they had been playing. Seizing a double handful, the man threw it full at the beast, where it exploded.

With a frantic leap, which carried it clear over the two humans, the creature capered off down the beach to the south-ward at a rate of which they hadn't believed it capable.

"Let's go," shouted Scarface, and gathering up their belong-ings, the two hurried off in the opposite direction.

They hadn't walked more than two or three hours when they came to a wide river flowing to the sea, and completely barring their path. But that didn't dismay them so much as the fact that near them, on their shore of the river, were the remnants of a cooking-fire!

It was bad enough to have to match their wits with the brute force of prehistoric monsters, but now they must contend with human intelligence as well; for this was no Viking land. The gangster searched among and around the charred embers for clews as to the type of beings who had camped there.

For a city-bred man, Scarface was developing into quite a woodsman. Necessity and a little experience can turn book-learning into real knowledge.

His search produced nothing, however, except two sizes of footprints.

"A cave man and his mate?" thought he. "But this is strange. We have seen no signs of any living creatures except mollusks, insects, fishes and toads. No mammals. No birds. Not even any reptiles. The trees are those of the coal age. I didn't know that man existed that long ago. This would certainly please the anti-evolutionists."

THE FOOTPRINTS led inland up the bank of the river; so Scarface decided that he and Borghild must cross the river at any cost; but when he investigated the edge of the stream, he found the thick mud literally swarming with smooth-skinned, lizard-like, venomous-appearing creatures, which made it evident that swimming was out of the question, and that even launching a raft would be attended by grave danger.

Meanwhile the girl too was examining the footprints. Suddenly she gave a little cry of surprise and discovery. Jimmy came running. Both knelt on the ground, as she pointed to something.

Near the moccasin prints was the unmistakable mark of a thoroughly modern shoe! This was even better than Bryan's prehistoric horseshoe. And then the truth dawned on them.

"Theresa!" they exclaimed in unison.

Therefore the moccasined prints were either those of Nils and Helga, or of savages who had captured little Terry. In either event, they must follow. So, picking up their belongings, Jimmy and Borghild hurried inland along the river trail.

The path was a well-defined animal track, winding in and out through otherwise impenetrable jungle, but keeping fairly close to the river's edge at all times. Jimmy still had his automatic, with one clip of cartridges, but no more, the rest of his armament having gone down with the Viking ship. So he carried this weapon in one hand, in readiness for instant use, though he doubted if it would be of much value against the small-brained creatures of this past age.

About a mile inland the road rose and topped a small and relatively bare hill, on the summit of which they found the three persons whom they sought. So the footprints had actually been those of Theresa Ferreira, Nils Uppri and Helga Redmond. Evolution was still unchallenged by prehistoric shoeprints!

Loud and warm were the greetings as the two groups embraced. Then Helga and Nils explained to Borghild, and Terry explained to Scarface Jimmy, that the three had been washed ashore on a piece of wreckage which had served as a raft. Despairing of finding any trace of their two companions, the three had at once proceeded northward, until blocked by the river, and then had turned inland, hoping to find a ford.

They had made a fire with Eric's old burning-glass which Helga carried. They were now engaged in building a stockade, to protect them from predatory beasts, until such time as they could devise some way of crossing the river.

"Gee, Mr. Jimmy," concluded Theresa, "we must teach these guys to talk United States. I'm all fed up on listening to Svenska."

But he shook his head, and replied, "No. It will be more useful for us to learn Norse, which will come in handy if we ever get back to the plateau city."

"Gee, Mr. Jimmy," said she, "you don't think we maybe gotter spend the rest of our lives in this dump, do you?"

"Perhaps," he replied. "Who knows?"

CHAPTER XIX

A PREHISTORIC SIEGE

IT WAS SOME job building a stockade, with knives as their only tools. But it had to be done, and so it was done. Until it was completed, some one always remained on guard while the others slept.

Then two roofed shelters were erected within the stockade, one for the women and the other for the men. A little spring bubbled from the ground within their inclosure; it was this that had determined the location. The smooth-skinned lizards of the river proved not bad eating, but their only vegetable was heart of palm, as they didn't dare try anything else.

By tacit agreement, Norse was the only language used, even between the two Americans, who rapidly mastered at least the rudiments of the ancient tongue. Scarface was most attentive to Borghild, and Nils to Theresa, while Helga acted as chaperon.

Their clothing rapidly became simplified. By pooling all their dress-goods, they were able to fashion two simple tunics apiece. Helga and Borghild did their hair in two long braids, and Terry looked forward to the time when her now-scraggly bob would permit her to do likewise. Jimmy let his beard continue to grow, a magnificent black mattress, which concealed most of his scar; but Nils, having little facial hair because of his youth and blondness, was able to keep fairly clean-shaved with a knife, except for his drooping yellow mustache. Scarface and Theresa dis-

carded their shoes and fashioned themselves moccasins and
Norse leggings out of lizard-hide.

Their days were fully employed: hunting, cooking, expeditions
to the sea for shell-fish and squid, strengthening their defens-
es, teaching and studying Norse—and making love. It was only
in the last-named pastime that Helga could not share. At such
times she was depressed, quite naturally, being separated hundreds or thousands of miles from her Eric. Were ships and
gliders searching for her, she wondered, or would he think her
dead? And, horrible thought, would he marry again? No wonder
the love-making of the others, who seemed not discontented
with this opportunity to get acquainted, rendered her gloomy.

They started building a large raft down at the beach, for they
figured that it would be impossible to cross the rivers of this
land, because of the slimy denizens of its mucky shores, but
that it should be feasible to paddle out to sea and follow the
shore.

One day one of the girls made an interesting discovery. For
a mirror they had all had to use a little pool in the brook, halfway
from the stockade to the river, and this was most inconvenient.
But now Helga noticed that the inner bark, where it peeled
dryly off one of the logs of the stockade, was shiny and silvery
like tinfoil. This gave her an idea. As time hung heavy on her
hands, she set about to put her discovery to practical use.

Finding another tree of the same species, she skinned some
of the inner bark and let it dry. But the result was disappoint-
ing, for it dried all crinkly and rumpled-up, like used tin-foil.

However, the girl noticed that it shrank as it dried, and this
gave her a further idea. She made a circular drum of palm-
branches, like an embroidery-hoop, and on this she stretched
some fresh inner bark. When this dried, it was taut and smooth,
and lo she had a mirror!

With these various occupations, days and perhaps weeks
wore on. The construction of a raft, and of paddles for it, was
nearly completed at the beach.

ONE TRAGIC morning, however, they awoke at cock-crow. Now, generally speaking, there is nothing strange or tragic in awakening in the morning at cock-crow. But in a land where there is no morning, but rather perpetual noonday with the sun always at the zenith, and where there are no cocks to crow, nor for that matter any other birds of any sort, such a combination of circumstances is a bit unusual, to say the least.

Of course, there was no actual morning; merely the time for arising from sleep. The sun shone squarely overhead as usual. But, as to the cock-crowing, there could be no mistake. They all heard it. The two Americans were used enough to the barnyard variety to recognize the sound.

The crowing which had disturbed them was answered from another quarter, and then there was silence. Hastily the five dressed, and mounted upon the platform which ran around the inside face of their palisade.

At first nothing was to be seen, but soon there emerged from the jungle the most peculiar gigantic fowl-like creature that any of them had ever beheld. It looked for all the world like a plucked chicken from a meat market, except that it towered all of ten feet high. It had thick slate-colored skin; small arms bearing claws, instead of wings; and no comb.

Stretching its neck aloft, and standing on tiptoe, the reptilian fowl proceeded to crow, with a voice that shook the earth. The challenge was answered by another stentorian crow from near by; and presently a second similar beast came upon the scene.

The two reptiles crouched low, stretched their necks toward each other, and teetered in unison for a moment; then suddenly, as at a signal, leaped into the air together, striking at each other with huge spurs which protruded from the inner sides of their legs. The little arms were not used.

"Gee, Mr. Jimmy," exclaimed little Terry, quite forgetting her duty to speak only Norse, "this is some cockfight!"

And so it was. The two creatures repeated their cycle of maneuvers over and over again, until one of them reeled backward upon the ground. Thereupon the other, disregarding all further formalities, kicked his prostrate foe about, until finally the body lay still. Then, standing in triumph upon the dead body, he gave one victorious crow, and waddled off.

The five spectators immediately shifted their interest from the thrill of battle to the prospect of a chicken dinner. Unbarring their gate, they rushed out and dragged the huge carcass within. But the victor, seeing his victim apparently alive and moving away from him, came running back with angry clucks, and nearly got in after his dead adversary, before they could close and bar the gate.

After a period of silence, Jimmy mounted the platform to see if the coast was clear again, and just barely escaped a vicious poke in the face from the giant gamecock, which had been standing quietly outside. The beast then stuck its head over the edge and tried to reach for Jimmy, who hastily scrambled down.

Thereafter, no one dared to get onto the platform, for fear of being pecked—and it would only take one peck from that great bill to kill a man.

But for the present the presence of their besieger didn't matter, as they busied themselves with cooking slices of his victim.

PRESENTLY they heard much clucking outside, and glancing through the cracks between the posts of their wall, they saw twenty or more similar giant fowl on the hill-top. But these new creatures had shorter necks and no spurs, and were rather stouter in build than the two who had fought.

The reptilian family settled down and made a regular ogres' farmyard out of the entire open space around the fort. They became more and more inquisitive as to what was inside, especially after devouring the offal from the slain rooster which was thrown outside. Not only did they keep craning over the top of the palisade, and snapping at any one who ventured upon the platform, but finally they took to pecking at any one who even tried to peek at them through the cracks. It was a state of siege.

The supply of heart of palm gave out. The remains of the chicken meat spoiled, and had to be thrown away. It soon became evident that they would have to fight or starve, so they called a council.

"We must try to make our way through them to the raft," announced Scarface. "Yet we may not survive to reach the shore. Before I die, I should like to marry Borghild. Can it not be arranged?"

"It can," replied Nils, "for I am not only a bishop, but also the head of her family. However, you have no man to act as your best friend and recount to me your deeds of prowess, in order to obtain my consent."

"Need it be a man?" asked the gangster.

"It always has been a man, since the beginning of our race," replied the Viking.

"But need it be?" insisted Scarface. "Is there any rule or law, other than mere custom, which compels it?"

"No-o," hesitated Nils.

"Then, Helga, quick! Be my sponsor."

Helga smiled. She remembered how she had sent Eric Redmond to Nils, when the latter was still a boy, to ask him to vouch for Eric to her father, the Bishop Thorvald.

She reminded Nils of that episode, and then launched into a panegyric, in which Scarface Boston Jimmy's tales of his World War adventures and career as a Chicago bootlegger—all strangely garbled—were made a foundation for his bravely risking his life in the Viking glider against Nick Fratelli, his defense of the Viking ship from pursuit, his rescue of the girl whom now he claimed, and his woodcraft and leadership in their present predicament.

It was a stirring saga, and all present were much impressed, not the least of them Jimmy himself. Nils gave his consent, and the nuptials were rushed, for there was no time to be lost if they would escape before starvation overcame them.

Thus Borghild Hoglund, the Viking maid, became Mrs. James Lefavour.

WHEN THE ceremony was over, Nils said, "I, too, wish to marry, if Theresa will have me. As bishop, I can ordain Jimmy to the Norse ministry, so that he can perform the sacrament. He is the nearest to a legal guardian that Terry has; and anyway, by virtue of being a bishop, I can appoint him to that position, too. Helga, will you sing a sister's praises of her brother, for Jimmy's ears to hear?"

Helga and Borghild smiled their approval. Scarface, however, was a bit appalled at the thought of himself, a bootlegger and gangster, receiving holy orders.

But little Terry interrupted. "Oh, Nils, I'm not sure, I'm not sure. Aren't we rushing into this merely because we may be about to die? Please give me time to think calmly."

Nils pleaded with her in vain; then at last he put his arms around her protectingly.

"I'll wait."

Scarface then outlined the plan of attack. They were to wrap their spare garments about their heads for protection. Each was to carry a stout stick. He would begin by trying to shoot the rooster. Then they were to fling open the gates, throw the coals of their cooking-fire at the hens, and run the gantlet to the beach.

So Scarface mounted the platform; and, as the cock's head appeared, he discharged his entire clip in its hideous face. Blinded and squawking, the beast rushed away, and tore around the inclosure like mad, finally dropping in his tracks.

Then the door was unbarred; and, as the female reptiles made a rush for it, hot coals were shoveled in their faces. They withdrew, squawking, for a short distance; but, when the five humans emerged, the hens rushed back at them again.

Beating the hens about the legs, and on the heads whenever they stooped to peck, the five prisoners fought their way onward. But something like the senseless persistency which causes a modern hen to run across the road in front of an automobile caused these prehistoric creatures to go perversely in the opposite direction from that in which they were being driven.

Gradually the progress of the five humans slowed down. Gradually they tired. At last Scarface gave the command to fall back toward the palisade again. Soon they were within its protecting walls, with the gate barred once more; trapped by carnivorous reptiles of a bygone age.

CHAPTER XX

THE RESCUE

THE DISCOURAGING FAILURE of their sortie against the creatures outside the stockade had plunged them all into hopeless melancholy. Scarface was glancing grimly at his useless "rod," when Terry burst out:

"Mr. Jimmy, listen!"

They could all hear a distant hum, as if of a motor.

"An airplane?" asked Terry, using the Viking word *skwaa* which had been applied to the plane in which the Radio Flyers had entered this world.

"No, my Eric's *skwaa* is out of 'gas,'" said Helga.

"Couldn't be the *Miami*, either," Jimmy pointed out. "They're out of gas, too."

Steadily the sound grew in volume.

"It *is* a plane!" shouted Scarface. "I can see it. Quick, smudge the fire, and attract its attention!"

But unluckily, the fire had all been used up in their fight with the reptiles, and not a spark remained. By the time that a new fire could be started, the airship would have passed by.

All five looked frantically around the inclosure for an idea.

"I have it!" shouted Scarface. "Heliograph!"

And he snatched Helga's bark mirror, and reflected the sunlight back up at the approaching craft. It was a chancy business; but finally he caught the pilot's attention. The plane circled, and began to descend.

"Saved! Saved!" they cried, embracing each other.

Yet how did they know that these flyers were friends? They were soon to find out.

There was room enough in the clearing, at the top of the knoll where stood their fort, for the plane to land, so it swooped, took the ground on its wheels—being equipped with wheels, skis and pontoons—and taxied almost to their very door. The great fowl-like reptiles scattered with fright at the roar of the motor, and the besieged party crowded onto the platform of the palisade.

From the plane disembarked two stalwart bearded Vikings in chain-mail and winged helmets. Helga gave one look at them, then opened the gate of the fortress and rushed out.

"Eric, my Eric," she sobbed, flinging herself into the arms of one of the aviators, "I knew you would come. I knew you would come."

The other Viking grinned.

"Hello, folks," said he in English.

It was Tom Jones, strangely metamorphosed.

"Gee, Mr. Jones," exclaimed Theresa. "I'd hardly of known you with your beard. You make a swell-looking Viking."

Eric Redmond then introduced Tom to Helga, and Helga introduced Eric to Scarface and Theresa. All was smiles and glad reunion, until Borghild announced to the two newcomers her recent marriage to Scarface Jimmy, whereupon Tom Jones's brow clouded.

"Any more marriages been taking place around here?" he asked rather truculently in Norse, glaring at young Nils.

"Alas, no," replied the boy bishop, squarely meeting the other's glance, "but I believe that it can be arranged."

He, the Bishop of Greenland, was not going to be patronized by a mere foreigner!

Helga smoothed the situation over by expressing amazement at the resuscitation of her Eric's long-dead plane.

"We owe it all to our new ally here," explained Eric, indicating Tom Jones. "We were drilling for water near the plateau and struck 'oil' instead. Tom used his scientific knowledge to 'distil' the oil and made 'gasoline,' so here we are."

"Great work," ejaculated Scarface.

"But how did you find *us?*" asked Helga.

"Quite simply," replied her husband. "You doubtless know that the *Miami* got out of gas. Skraeling canoes towed her ashore, where we later captured her. All the *Miami's* crew escaped us except Charley Loy. The Skraeling rifle corps made good their retreat, with their rifles and ammunition. They are a decided menace. However, we have the *Miami's* machine guns. Altoonah is dead, as you may not know."

"We ought to know," said Scarface, and explained their adventure.

"YOU HAVEN'T yet told us how you found us," persisted Helga.

"As soon as we learned of your escape, from a Skraeling prisoner," explained her husband, "we assumed that you had been blown south in the storm, so we scoured the sea with dragon ships further south than Vikings had ever ventured before. But we found no trace of you. Not even any wreckage of Nils's ship, which fact encouraged us. So the moment this plane was reconditioned, Jones and I set out to skirt the entire shore of this new southern sea."

During all this conversation, the reptilian hens had gradually been edging nearer, so Tom Jones gave the motor a whir, and they all scattered again precipitately.

"We can take only one of you back with us now," announced Eric, "and that must be one of the ladies. You can choose between you. Then either Jones or I will make a couple of trips alone and bring the others back by twos. How are you off for provisions?"

The recently besieged party explained that they were starving, so while Tom taxied the plane around the clearing to keep the

*It was a fearful task to push the plane
across that infernal valley.*

besieging beasts away, the rest dragged in the body of the dead rooster, and gathered a quantity of palm-hearts.

Meanwhile the three girls had decided that little Terry, being from the outside world and the youngest should be the first passenger.

When this was announced, Nils promptly objected.

"I won't have her leaving here with that Jones fellow!" he exclaimed.

Every one was surprised at this outburst. But, because he was their bishop, his wishes were respected. After some discussion, it was finally agreed that Tom, Nils, and Theresa were to fly to the plateau together, and then have Angus Selkirk bring back the plane.

The plane departed, and the besieging reptiles closed around the two married couples, Eric and Helga, Scarface and Borghild, in the stockade.

In due course of time, Angus Selkirk arrived with the plane again. Then Eric flew the two girls back, leaving Angus and Scarface alone in the fort.

But when Eric reached the plateau city, he found that the boy bishop, taking advantage of the absence of the two *yarls*, had thrown Tom Jones into prison, and was forcing his attentions onto Theresa, despite her growing objections. Eric remonstrated with him, but in vain.

Eric was very anxious to get Tom out of jail and conciliate him, for Tom was a tremendous scientific acquisition for the Viking civilization. So the *yarl* cleverly suggested that Tom, rather than he, fly back to the stockade, to get Angus and Scarface.

"Very well," agreed Nils, "and I hope he crashes."

To Eric's surprise, Tom gladly agreed to leave the plateau city; and during his absence, Nils appeared to be making great progress with Theresa. It seemed that she was piqued with the willingness with which Tom had left her.

Meanwhile, in the cabin far to the southward, Angus and Scarface were rapidly becoming acquainted. The Scotch *yarl* of the Vikings had harbored a sneaking admiration for the Chicago man, ever since that day in the assembly hall of the plateau city, when the latter, unarmed and a prisoner, had boldly faced his captors, and had dictated terms to them instead of suing for mercy.

The two men had much in common. They were by far the two most forceful characters of the whole civilized population of the underworld.

In due course, Tom Jones arrived with the plane, and the three men bade a last farewell to the little cabin. Then they started northward. But a storm drove them to the west, and finally forced them to land, and stake down their plane.

CHAPTER XXI

THE FATAL MAGNET

WHEN THE CENTRAL sun shone forth again through the clouds, they started north once more.

They had been but a short time on the wing, when they saw far to the left of them a barren rocky desert, and beyond that an encampment of tents.

"Let's reconnoiter," suggested Angus. "That may be Nick Fratelli and his Skraelings. We have been unable to locate them ever since we routed them, and drove them south."

So the plane headed for the desolate valley.

But scarcely had they winged over its edge, when their motor started coughing and sputtering, and the plane seemed strangely nose-heavy.

"Not out of gas, I hope?" inquired Scarface anxiously.

Tom Jones cocked his ear, and listened intently.

"N-n-no," he replied judiciously. "The gauge shows nearly full, although that isn't any proof. It sounds like ignition trouble. It's as though the ignition were all right in itself, but were struggling against something that is trying to interfere with it."

The engines sputtered a few times more, and then stopped completely, Jones headed down, and made a pancake landing; but the plane did not bounce—it hit with a jar, and rolled along as if glued to earth.

As their ship came to a stop, they examined the gas-tanks, which were almost full; then Tom and Angus went over the wiring, which seemed all right.

But when he brought out the pocket voltmeter to test the wiring, the little instrument behaved most queerly. It did not appear to be broken, and yet the needle registered a high voltage, without any current being connected up at all.

As they worked, they all kept hitching up their belts. They did it subconsciously, hardly noticing that they were doing so, until Scarface, who not being an electrical expert, wasn't so engrossed as the two others, remarked, "What the devil is the matter with my gat? It seems heavy as lead."

He took it from his holster, and immediately it was nearly wrenched from his hand by some invisible downward pull.

"Why, it weighs a ton!" he gasped, stooping to lay the weapon on the ground.

As the pistol neared the rocky floor of the valley it was jerked downward, and struck the ground with a click. Scarface tried to lift it again, but it stuck to the ground as though glued there. He found, however, that he could quite easily slide it along the surface.

Selkirk and Jones had knocked off work to watch the performance. Each took out his own gun, and went through the same experience. Their faces were wrapped in puzzled frowns. Then suddenly the light dawned on them.

"I have it!" exclaimed Tom. "Lodestone! This whole valley is made of lodestone, magnetic iron ore. That's what put our ignition out of kilter."

"If you're right," said Angus, "the only way we can ever get out of here is to wheel our plane out of this valley. The bank to the west looks less steep. Let's get going."

"How do you know which way is west?" asked Scarface.

"Because we were headed west when we crashed," explained the *yarl*.

"But how did you head west in the first place?" persisted the other.

"Gyroscopic compass."

"Oh, so you have one of those newfangled things, same as we did on the *Miami*. Well, let's go."

They started pushing the plane westward. It was an arduous task. Just merely pushing the plane wasn't so bad, but the floor of the valley was strewn with bowlders of all sizes, and was pitted with holes. Some of the smaller bowlders they could and did move out of their way. Some of the smaller pits they could and did fill with stones. But the larger bowlders and holes they had to go around; and often, after making considerable progress, they would reach an impasse and have to back up and lose all that they had gained. This was most discouraging.

THE PLACE was weird and oppressive. On all sides stretched the bare magnetic ore. The many pits in its surface gave it a lunar appearance. There was no soil, and hence no plant life. There were no animals, not even any insects. Of course there were no birds, for birds are not found that far south within the earth. Even the winged lizards gave the place a wide berth. Was it some sixth sense, unpossessed by humans, that enabled the pterodactyls and insects to feel the magnetic emanations, or was it merely the desolation that drove them away?

The heat was intense. The central sun beat pitilessly down. The metallic rocks absorbed the heat until they were like the top of a stove. The air trembled and writhed as it rose from the hot surface, distorting the shape of the surrounding hills. But luckily this very rising of the air sucked in cooler air from all sides, and thus created a slight breeze, which was all that made the awful valley bearable.

Even so, the three men quickly stripped off practically all of their already scant primitive garments, except their sandals, and stowed the discarded clothes in the cockpit. The pistol-belts had long since been removed, because of the magnetic weight of the pistols.

"This is worse than Death Valley!" exclaimed Tom.

"It is that!" assented Angus, puffing from his exertions.

"Never been there, but I can well believe it," added Jimmy.

The sweat poured down their muscular bodies, as they struggled on. So intent were they on their work that they didn't notice anything particular going on around them, until a rifle cracked ahead of them. At the same instant a splinter flew from one of the struts of the plane, striking Angus in the cheek.

"Duck!" he cried, and plunged behind a nearby bowlder.

But the others needed no command. Scarface, from long experience, had automatically taken to cover almost before the shot reached them, and Tom Jones was quick to follow suit.

"It's Nick the Rat, and his Skraelings!" exclaimed Scarface grimly. "And all our guns are in the airplane. Curse the luck!"

"The top of the cliff wabbles in this heated air so badly that I can hardly see what's there," replied Angus, "but I guess it's them all right."

"Lucky for you it does, old man," asserted Tom. "If it hadn't been as hard for them to see us, as it is for us to see them, you'd have been hit."

"How'll we get our guns?" asked Angus. "I don't fancy standing up again and being potted. And we can't reach the cockpit without standing up."

"I tell you," announced Tom. "First, do you think they know how many of us there are?"

"I doubt it," replied Angus. "We've kept pretty close to the plane all the time, so that our outlines, in this wiggly heat, must have blended into it pretty well."

"Then suppose you and Jimmy start off south as conspicuously as possible, as though you were trying to escape. Draw their fire from time to time by standing up when running from cover to cover."

"Sounds like a book," interrupted Scarface, grinning.

"Well, then, let's hope they read it wrong," replied Angus.

"Nick never was much of a hand at reading," added Scarface. "Go on, Tom. What's the rest of your plan?"

The boy made a gesture of impatience at all this levity.

"When you get quite a way from the ship," he continued, "I shall try to sneak into the cockpit and get our guns. Then you can crawl back, really keeping under cover, and we shall be armed to defend ourselves."

"Come on then," agreed Angus.

"It's jake with me," confirmed Scarface.

Suddenly arising to his feet, he sped southward across the meteoric floor of the valley. A perfect volley of shots resulted from the cliff to the west. He dropped behind a bowlder.

"Are you all right?" called Angus.

"Never touched me," came back the cheery reply.

This interchange of shouts brought several more shots from the enemy, some directed at Scarface's bowlder and some at the plane.

Tom whispered to Angus. "This shows that there mustn't be any hollering back and forth after you get away from here. The acoustics are too good."

"Glad there's something that's good about this infernal place. Well, here I go. Watch me!"

And, amid another volley of shots, he dashed across the open, and joined Jimmy.

From then on, the two were a bit more cautious, and yet they made certain, each time they moved, to be conspicuous enough to draw fire.

Draw fire they did, and even had one or two very narrow escapes, in spite of the waviness of the atmosphere.

WHEN THEY were well on their way, Tom sneaked carefully around to the end of the tail. No shots resulted. Quite evidently he had not been seen. He stood up by the rudder. Now he could see the cliff-top, but they did not see him. His figure must have blended with that of the ship, for no bullets came his way.

The firing continued, and at every shot, Tom would jerk nervously; but the bullets were apparently directed at his two companions.

Slowly, almost imperceptibly, he crawled up over the elevators, and then wormed his way along the top of the tail, until he dropped into the cockpit with a gasp of relief.

Scarface and Angus were still dodging from rock to rock, inviting potshots, but no one had yet noticed Tom's maneuver. One by one, he took out the precious rifles, and lowered them slowly over the side with a loop of rope. Quite a job, on account of the magnetic attraction. But he accomplished it without any tell-tale clatter.

The three pistol belts followed, with equal success.

Just as he was about to crawl back along the tail again, the thought suddenly occurred to him, "Why all the precautions now? I've got the firearms out. Why not jump, and run for a rock?"

But then he decided that the less the enemy knew, the better, even if he couldn't see any particular harm in giving them any particular bit of information. So back along the tail he crawled.

Halfway there he slipped. Groping quickly for a handhold threw him still further off his balance, and he slid clattering off the plane, to land with a thud on the metallic ground beneath.

A volley of shots spattered about the plane.

"Are you all right, Tom?" shouted Scarface and Angus in unison.

But poor Tom made no reply.

"Stay here!" exclaimed Scarface to Angus. "No need of both of us getting bumped off."

So saying, he sprang up from the rock behind which he was taking cover, and raced across the open toward where Tom lay motionless on the ground by the tail of the plane.

Meanwhile Angus started crawling cautiously back toward the plane.

The element of surprise in Scarface's dash was probably all that saved him from annihilation. He was halfway to his goal before the enemy opened fire, and he reached it without mishap, dropping beside Tom.

Angus did not dare to shout and ask if Scarface were hit, for that would reveal his own whereabouts. Nor did Scarface dare shout to reassure him. So both kept quiet, and Angus continued his crawl.

There was not much cover where the two lay by the plane, so Scarface, after catching his breath, dragged Tom's body behind a near-by bowlder. This brought another volley; but no casualties. Then he searched the body for bullet wounds; but none were evident. He placed his ear on the other's chest; the heart still beat. Tom was only stunned.

THERE was no water to throw in his face to revive him. The heat was intense; even Scarface was reeling with it. However, he chafed the other's wrists and ankles, and finally brought him round.

"Where am I?" asked Tom, sitting up weakly.

"In Death Valley, still," replied Scarface grimly. "How do you feel?"

"Hot as hell," replied Jones, "but otherwise okeh."

Just then Angus joined them.

After inquiring for the health of both of them, he said: "I've an idea. Your friend Nick and his Skraelings never fired at me once on my way back here. If I can crawl in one direction without being seen, I can crawl in the other. So can one of you. Let's two of us crawl in opposite directions to the cliff, get up over the edge somehow, take cover on the top, flank them, and open fire. Try to pot Nick. If we succeed, the leaderless natives will run.

"The one of us who stays at the plane—and I think it had better be Jones, because he's still a bit weak—can crawl back and forth from rock to rock near by here, and fire an occasional shot from different spots, to make them think we are all still here. What do you say?"

It was an unusually long speech for the taciturn Scot. He never spoke without thinking, but this plan he had carefully thought out.

Scarface approved at once. Tom demurred at playing the least dangerous part on the program, but finally yielded to the insistence of the two others. To mollify him, they permitted him to sneak out and drag in the firearms.

They had completely forgotten the magnetic nature of their surroundings. But when they came to pick up their rifles and automatics, preparatory to setting forth, the lodestone was brought forcibly to their attention again.

"How the devil are we going to carry several tons of firearms with us?" exclaimed Scarface, exasperated.

"We've just got to, that's all," sighed Angus.

So they started out, one to the right, and the other to the left, dragging their guns with difficulty, while Tom crawled from bowlder to bowlder around the plane, firing from time to time at the cliff. At first he planned to fire from three different locations, thus simulating the three of them; but then it occurred to him that, if he used six or eight locations, he might be able to give the impression that the plane had carried quite a large force.

Unfortunately he overdid it. Nick had become quite certain that there were only three men confronting him, but he had been too cowardly to make a direct attack on even only three. He saw through Tom's ruse at once. In fact he got a glimpse of Tom on one of his crawls, and nearly potted him. And then he searched for and located the other two.

Tom Jones sat behind a bowlder and bandaged a bad nick in his left upper arm. If it hadn't been for the wavy atmosphere they might have got him that time. Several more shots rang out, but no bullets spattered near. Far to one side he could see Scarface lying low, behind a rock; he must be their target now.

Tom turned to look at Angus, who was just then worming his way out from behind some cover. Another fusillade from the cliff-top, and then Angus leaped in the air with a yell of pain and collapsed behind a bowlder.

Tom heard a cheer in front of him, and peering out from behind his protecting rock, he saw the Skraelings charging down over the face of the bank, brandishing their rifles as they came.

Coolly steadying his heavy and unwieldy piece on the rock before him, Tom opened fire on the oncoming enemy. Far to one side, Scarface Boston Jimmy did the same.

But as the Skraelings reached the bottom of the bank, a surprising thing happened. Their rifles were snatched from their hands by some unseen force, and fell clattering to the ground.

Several of them bolted back up the face of the bank. Several more fell before the bullets of the lone two who were opposing them. The rest stooped to pick up their fallen weapons again, and found to their horror that the rifles had suddenly and inexplicably become so heavy that they could scarcely be budged.

AS THE Skraeling horde paused irresolute at the foot of the cliff, with their leaders urging them on, although almost as astonished as they, the motionless central sun was darkened by a cloud. And then the rain fell in torrents.

Each crowd was blotted from the other's sight by the descending deluge. All was dark as night, the only night ever known to this central world, the night of a tropical tempest.

The thunder roared like an artillery barrage. The lightning flashed almost continually, and yet did not serve to illumine the scene appreciably, so thick was the falling rain.

Neither Tom Jones nor Scarface Jimmy sought shelter from the downpour. So parched and feverish were they from the sweltering heat of the awful valley that they both welcomed the refreshing rain. It soothed and cooled them, in spite of its driving force. They scooped up and drank the water which collected in hollows in the rocky floor of the valley. They were filled with renewed life and pep.

But not so the enemy. The Skraelings had been living in comfort in the jungle near by, and were in no need of cooling water. To them, the cloudburst was merely another calamity added to the ghostly snatching of their rifles, and the inexplicable weight which those weapons had suddenly acquired.

So when the storm finally lifted, Tom and Scarface were all set to renew the fray, with rifles propped against sheltering bowlders, whereas the majority of the Skraelings were frantically scrambling up the slippery side of the cañon, their firearms for the most part abandoned at the bottom.

The rain had cleared the air and cooled the rocks. No longer did the valley glow with unbearable furnace heat. No longer did rising heat waves distort the appearance of all objects into wiggly lines. Everything looked clear and normal; and as soon as the last drop had fallen, and the light of the red central sun again showed through the scurrying clouds, the two young Americans began to pick off the scrambling Skraelings one by one with unerring accuracy. Almost every shot told.

Among the naked savages, certain leaders could be seen urging them to return to the attack. At these leaders, therefore, the two marksmen directed their first shots, and soon had the satisfaction of eliminating every one of them. But, because these leaders were clothed—or rather unclothed—exactly like their followers, it was impossible to make out which, if any, of them was the hated Nick Fratelli. For Nick, with his World War experience, had had the sense not to garb himself in Viking armor, as had been the custom among the Skraeling chiefs who had preceded him. Thus he saved himself from becoming the conspicuous target that he otherwise would have been.

Nor could the two marksmen tell whether the enemy leaders whom they had brought down had been hit, or merely had been driven to take cover.

The now leaderless Skraelings abandoned their futile attempt to scale the slippery cliff. Some took cover at the foot, but by far the larger part of their number turned and fled precipitately southward around the interior edge of the valley. Many lay dead or dying.

Scarface signaled to Tom, and the two at once began a steady crawl from rock to rock, converging toward the enemy position, their common idea being to gain possession of the deserted rifles, before the Skraelings could recover sufficient morale to attack them again in force. For even the remaining handful of the enemy would be more than a match for the two Americans, if only the Skraelings would get together again and act with courage.

But apparently a very similar idea had occurred to some of those on the other side, for as Scarface Jimmy was crawling cautiously around a large rock about halfway to the foot of the cliff, he almost bumped his head against that of Nick the Rat.

Instantly the two men staggered to their feet, and raised their rifles to fire. But they had forgotten the magnetic pull of the lodestone ground, which resisted this movement. The rifles stayed down, and nearly upset both men in their efforts to lift them so precipitately.

SCARFACE was the first to size up the situation. Letting go his rifle, which rushed with a clatter to the rocky floor, he grabbed for his automatic. But his opponent, instantly sensing the movement, flung himself upon him. Grappling, the two went down.

The clatter of Jimmy's rifle, as it fell, attracted the attention of Tom Jones. Raising his own rifle and resting its great weight upon a rock, he drew a careful bead upon the struggling pair, and calmly waited for an opportunity to fire at the Italian without endangering his friend.

At last the opportunity offered. Tom gave a rapid but steady squeeze on the trigger. But just as the firing-pin clicked into place, and the shot roared forth, a heavy form flung itself from

behind upon the unsuspecting Tom. The bullet struck harmlessly just to one side of the wrestlers.

Tom tried to wrench his gun around toward his assailant,
but the magnetic pull prevented thus sudden a movement, so
he turned and swung his fist at the man who was grappling
with him. The man staggered back, and Tom sprang to his feet
and faced him.

It was Cicero Tony Schultz!

For a moment they confronted each other glaring. Then, as
if suddenly inspired by a common thought, each drew his automatic and fired.

But both entirely failed to take into account that fatal magnetic pull. Even Billy the Kid in his palmiest days couldn't have
been "quick on the draw" with a hundred-pound six-gun.

Before firing a second time, each clapped his left hand
beneath his right hand and lifted with all his force.

It was a cold-blooded performance, standing there within a
few paces of each other, each with both feet firmly braced, and
both hands employed in trying to lift a massive piece of ord-
nance—about four inches long—into position to annihilate the
other.

Both fired simultaneously, and Tom Jones dropped his gun
with a cry. His right arm hung limp.

Cicero still held his heavy gun in both hands, steadying it to
fire again. He stepped backward several paces. Tom stood for
a moment, bewildered by his wound; then flung himself on his
enemy.

Tom realized that he was leaping to his death, but it was his
one and only chance. Some trick of fate might stay the bullet
of the Dutchman until Tom could reach him and strike him
with his intact left fist. His right arm was useless.

The imminence of death speeded Jones's perceptions to an
unbelievable degree. Just as the whole past life of a drowning
man is supposed to flash before his eyes as he goes down, so
time was distorted for Tom Jones during the brief instant in

which he sprang across the space which separated him from Cicero Tony.

So stimulated was his mind, that it seemed as though he were taking part in a slow-motion picture. He saw, as in a nightmare, the other man swing the muzzle of the automatic steadily toward his heart.

A sneer played over the features of his executioner. Cicero wanted to be so very sure that his aim was true, before he pulled the trigger.

Then came a flash and a roar! But Tom felt no pain, no stunning blow. And yet it could not be that the other had missed at that short distance.

As the two crashed to the ground together, Tom's mind, still working with lightning-like speed, recalled the stories he had read of the Moros of the Philippines, who, although shot through the heart at fifty yards by American soldiers, would still keep on coming, and would bury their curved knives in the vitals of their slayers.

But it was to meet just that situation that the forty-fives had been invented. A forty-five would not only *kill* at fifty paces, but the impact of its bullet would stop a man in his tracks and drop him at the very spot where he was when hit. And Cicero was armed with a forty-five! Why then had Tom been able to keep on?

With this thought flashing through his mind, Tom's left hand clutched his enemy's throat.

But a calm voice behind him said, "Lay off him, Tom, he's dead."

And Angus Selkirk leaned down and pulled the youth off his victim.

Bewildered, Tom staggered to his feet and looked around. Angus stood beside him, an automatic in one hand.

"But I was killed!" exclaimed Jones inanely, not yet realizing that it was Selkirk's shot which he had heard, and that Cicero had delayed his trigger-finger an instant too long.

"About the way I was," replied the Scot grinning, "until the rain brought me out of it, just in time…. Say, see what's going on over there." Tom turned.

JIMMY and his former lieutenant were confronting each other with clenched fists.

"You're facing the middleweight champion of Chicago," taunted Nick, "and you've made the last wisecrack about me that you're ever going to make. Come on and take your medicine!"

Scarface saved his breath, and drove at the other's chest with his right fist. The Italian gave way a step, and lunged straight at Jimmy's face. But Jimmy swayed a bit to one side, tilted his head a bit further, and then drove square at Nick's oncoming chin.

The impact threw the Italian off his balance. Up went both hands to steady himself. He was completely unguarded.

Jimmy was too eager to take advantage of the situation. He swung viciously—and missed! He fanned the air as his feet skidded on the rain-wet rocks.

But so did Nick's. The two men toppled over together.

Jimmy, cat-like, was on his feet again in an instant, but his opponent lay stunned. Out flashed Jimmy's automatic from beneath his left armpit, but was nearly wrenched from the hand that held it by the tremendous pull of the magnetic rocks.

"Stop!" thundered Angus. "Take him alive! The Althing—the council—will deal with him."

So Scarface grabbed his gun in both hands and stood over the prostrate figure, ready and waiting for any hostile move.

But none came. Nick's body lay limp and still.

Tom and Angus hurried over; and while the two others stood guard, Tom dropped to his knees and put his head to the fallen man's chest. Not a sound. He pulled the body to one side, and the head wabbled loosely and disconnectedly.

"Neck broken," asserted Scarface. Then, with a bit of his old-time Napoleonic braggadocio, *"Sic semper* Fratelli."

"Why, you're using your right arm!" exclaimed Angus to Tom.

"So I am," replied Tom, in surprise.

Then, raising it he inspected it carefully for signs of a wound. Blood was dripping from the elbow.

"I guess it nicked my crazy-bone, that's all," said he.

A shot from the cliff startled them. Instantly the three dropped to cover. Then they peered cautiously out.

From behind a bowlder by the foot of the cliff there projected a Skraeling rifle.

Angus carefully drew a bead, and fired. The bullet almost nicked the other's gun, but did no harm to the Skraeling himself.

"He'll keep his head down for a while now," remarked Scarface Jimmy grimly.

Tom Jones picked up a small round piece of lodestone about the size of a baseball.

"What we need," said he, "is mortar-fire."

Whereupon he heaved the rock at the hiding enemy. It described a graceful parabola, and landed neatly on the Skraeling's rifle, as Tom had known it would. His two companions followed suit.

There came a howl of surprise and pain, and then not one Skraeling, but rather four, leaped from their cover and bolted south.

The three Americans watched them go. The fleeing men had left their rifles behind, and were not worth firing at. They ran for a hundred yards or so, until they came to a low and rather gently sloping part of the bank, up which they scrambled, and soon disappeared into the jungle beyond.

"That's just the place to roll out our airplane!" exclaimed Angus. "Come on."

The tropical central sun was now beating down on them again with full force. The cloud remnants of the recent storm had long since departed. The rain-water in the pitted holes of the magnetic valley was steaming skyward. The air was becoming insufferably hot again.

"First we must bury poor old Nick," asserted Scarface.

"Bury *him!*" exclaimed Angus in disgust. "Let's feed him to the hyænodonts!"

But Scarface emphatically shook his head.

Said he, "Nick the Rat was my partner and my pal and my right-hand man for years. You two have known him only at his worst. But I remember him as he was before Cicero Schultz poisoned his mind. For old times' sake, I am going to bury him."

"But we have no shovels," objected Tom.

"And the jungle beasts will dig him up anyhow," added Angus. "That's why we always sail our Viking dead out to sea, on a burning raft or ship."

"Then let's bury him here in Death Valley, where the beasts never come," suggested Jimmy.

So together the three men rolled the body into the deepest hole in the metallic surface of the valley's floor, and then piled the hole full of rocks, on top of the body.

Similar burial they gave to Cicero Tony Schultz, not out of any love or respect, nor even for old times' sake, but merely because, after all, he had been an American like themselves.

AMID SWELTERING heat, they proceeded to roll their crippled aircraft to the low spot in the cliff. But they could not get her up the incline. It was too muddy and too steep.

So they dragged out the rifles—some job, with the magnetic rocks trying to pull them back—and made camp to await the drying of the incline.

Some small game was shot, and rain-water was fetched from the valley. Then they slept for uncounted hours. Time meant nothing in this land of the central sun.

They had a strange awakening. From some bushes a little way inland from the cliff-top, there appeared two long swan-like necks, each topped by a reptilian head.

"Great Scott, what a snake!" exclaimed Tom.

"I don't blame you for thinking so," said Angus, "but those are dobrats."

"What?" asked Tom.

"Dobrats."

"And what are dobrats?"

"A kind of prehistoric reptile. I think the scientists call them iguanodons."

At just that moment the two beasts waddled out into the open, directly toward the camp. They stood about fifteen feet high. Their hindquarters were heavy, their tails and hind legs muscular, their shoulders narrow, and their fore legs puny. The general effect was like kangaroos except that these reptiles walked rather than hopped.

Tom and Jimmy sprang to their feet and snatched up their rifles. The beasts saw them, but appeared to be neither enraged nor frightened.

"Don't shoot!" admonished Angus. "They're perfectly harmless. Not much good to eat, but their eggs are delicious."

"Fancy eating dinosaur eggs!" exclaimed Tom, laying down his rifle and studying the two creatures. "Wouldn't Ray Chapman Andrews be thrilled!"

The dobrats stopped at a tall bush quite near the men's camp, and started browsing off the top leaves. But suddenly they ceased their feeding, and became alert, gazing this way and that with evident apprehension. And then, without warning, a third beast, very similar to the other two except that its head was larger and its neck shorter and more sturdy, charged out of the woods with a roar. The dobrats scattered.

"A man-eater!" cried Angus.

The three men promptly raced for a near-by tree, and boosted and hauled each other up into its branches. When they were safely ensconced thirty feet or so above the ground, they looked down. The tyrannosaurus, or allosaur, or whatever it was, was perched on the back of one of the dobrats, and had borne it to the ground. The captor's jaws were clamped about its victim's neck.

With a wrench, the head was severed. Then the huge carnivore began to feast on its victim. At various spots in the distant sky several small black specks appeared, and rapidly converged, growing larger as they came. They were winged lizards the size of crows, the buzzards of that prehistoric world. On their arrival, they perched on near-by trees, awaiting their turn at the feast.

One of these pterosaurs, becoming a bit impatient for its share of the carcass of the dobrat, circled the feasting beast; but a sudden lift of the latter's head and a snap from its jaws, and the little bat-like creature dropped crushed and quivering to the ground. With a growl, the huge beast resumed its eating, tearing great pieces of flesh from the body of its kill, and gulping them down without chewing.

The three men watched, fascinated.

NOW THE surrounding underbrush began to rustle and shake with the motion of unseen forms, one of which finally emerged. It was a long and narrow beast, with high arched back, covered with horny plates. Its legs were stocky, its head abnormally small. But its most remarkable feature was the bunch of spikes, like a Viking war-club, in which its tail terminated.

"A stegosaurus, I'll bet!" exclaimed Tom.

Whatever it was, it cautiously and tentatively approached the carcass. The feasting reptile raised its head and growled. But the spiked one, unheeding, snatched a piece of meat. At that, the killer of the carcass sprang suddenly on the other's back. But he could not get either his claws or his teeth through the heavy armor-plates. And then the clubbed tail was brought into play, until finally the original attacker was driven off.

The other, also somewhat mauled, in spite of its armor, retired into the bushes. The feaster returned to gorge undisturbed.

Tom and Scarface had brought their rifles with them in their flight. Scarface now drew a careful bead on the huge prehistoric reptile, and fired. The bullet struck the creature's head. But the beast merely scratched fumblingly at the place with one forepaw for a moment, as though annoyed by an insect, and then resumed eating.

Said Tom, "That huge head has probably only a spoonful of brains. It will take a better shot than that, to reach a vital spot."

So they didn't fire again.

At last the beast satisfied his appetite and waddled off. The bat-winged lizards flapped down from the tree-tops and perched on what was left of the poor dobrat. Smaller reptiles emerged from the bushes, and contested for the remains. The three men clambered out of the tree, picked up their camp, and hastened down into the valley to their plane.

CHAPTER XXII

CONSPIRACY

"THIS IS NO place for us!" exclaimed Angus, pointing out the obvious.

"But we can't move our ship without a block-and-tackle," objected Tom, "and we haven't one."

"We have plenty of rope, though," contributed Jimmy, "and we can whittle out pulleys if we have to."

"Take too long," objected Angus. "We've got to get out of here. A winch would be easier than pulleys."

"Let's make a winch then," suggested Tom. "Come on."

Under his guidance, they cut down a tree about eight inches thick, and cut off a log about six feet long, with three pieces of branch projecting at almost right angles from one end.

Just beyond the top of the incline, up which they had been trying to push the airplane, there stood two trees five feet apart. From these trees the men trimmed all the low branches, except one on each, projecting away from the valley at a height of about four feet above the ground.

Into the crotches thus formed, they lifted their log. The rope, hitched to the bow of the plane, was secured to this log. Then they took turns, two of them at the handles of the winch thus formed, while the third chocked the wheels of the plane to keep it from sliding back.

It was hard work, but the plane actually moved, and soon was out of the awful magnetic valley. To their delight, they found that the motor functioned perfectly again, now that it was beyond the influence of the lodestones.

Some further time was consumed in wheeling the craft, with assistance from its whirling propellers, until they finally jockeyed it into an open space large enough for a take-off.

But before they left, they carried off all the Skraeling rifles, forty-three in number, cached them beside a large rock in the jungle, where they could easily be found again. For the rifles would have been too heavy a load for their plane to carry, in addition to the three men.

The reptiles and the little *skwaas* were just picking the last shreds of meat from the white bones of the dobrat, as the three men soared up and away to the northward once more.

The rest of the flight home was uneventful, and soon they landed, amid stirred-up clouds of red pollen, in the fields which flanked the plateau of the Viking city.

Great was the rejoicing at their return, for they had delayed so long *en route* that every one had begun to worry about them. And even greater was the rejoicing, when it was learned that Nick Fratelli and Cicero Tony Schultz would menace them no more. The power of the enemy was broken forever. Leaderless and nearly weaponless, they had now been driven further from the Viking strongholds than ever before.

During their absence, Nils, the boy bishop, had dug up the body of Captain Ferreira and had given it a stupendous flaming Viking burial at sea, in an endeavor to make an impression on little Terry. The girl did seem impressed, and Nils appeared to have made so much progress with her that he scorned to make any hostile move toward Tom on the latter's return.

Terry had suppressed her anxiety at Tom's long delay, and now Tom made no effort to see her, much as he desired to. Poor chap! The loving reunion of Jimmy with Borghild, and Angus with Astrid, made him lonely.

After a rest, he and Angus each took one trip back to bring
in the rifles, while preparations were made on the plateau for
a big celebration of their final victory over the Skraelings.

GREAT preparations were made for the celebration of the
Skraelings' downfall. A huge banquet was held in the assembly
hall. Theresa Ferreira occupied the place of honor at the right
hand of Bishop Nils. Almost every one regarded them as practically betrothed.

Upon Scarface, Nils bestowed the rank of *yarl*. Tom Jones,
Mike Murphy, Little Arty, and even Charley Loy were knight-
ed. Otho the Silver-tongued, *yarl* of a distant city, sang a saga,
especially composed for the occasion, in which he recounted,
madly garbled, the cruise of the *Miami*, and the other adventures of the new Yarl *Fee-ess-med-air*, which is Norse for "Scarface."

Speeches were made, in the boisterous language of the
Vikings, by Nils and Eric and Angus. And then the bishop
called on Scarface Boston Jimmy for a few remarks.

The new *yarl* thanked them for the honor which they had
bestowed upon him, and expressed his appreciation of having
had the opportunity of battling side by side with them against
the common enemy, and his regret at ever having conspired
against them.

"And now," he concluded in broken Norse, "you doubtless
wish to know where I plan to settle, for as a true Viking I assume
that you will give me no lands, but rather will send me forth to
conquer my own yarldom.

"Two hundred miles to the northeastward, where your glider
first sighted us when we invaded the center of the earth, there
is a peninsula which I surveyed from a mountain top. At that
time it appealed to me. I visioned it netted with roads and
dotted with teeming cities. I stamped my foot on the summit,
and took possession in my own name. The surrounding country
seemed uninhabited, even by Skraelings. The general appearance
is more like the outer earth than these lands here to the south-

ward. So if you will give me men and barges, I will go and colonize that peninsula, and establish there my yarldom."

His Borghild beamed with pride.

He struck his sword on the rough board table, for he was garbed as a Viking of the Vikings, and shouted, "Who will volunteer to sail in the fleet of James Lefavour?"

"I will!" cried Tom Jones, springing to his feet.

"And so will I," cried Little Arty.

"And I," added Mike Murphy.

"And I. And I. And I," chimed in Vikings from all over the hall.

Bishop Nils smiled with approval, and pressed Theresa's hand. His rival, Tom Jones, had been the first to volunteer in this new adventure, from which he might never return.

When the commotion was over Tom obtained the floor and suggested that, after the next sleep, he and Scarface should fly up to the new yarldom to reconnoiter. And the bishop smiled again, and hastened to approve.

The next morning quite a crowd came down to see them off. Eric and his wife Helga. Angus and his wife Astrid. Borghild to bid godspeed to her Yimmy. Nils and Theresa, arm in arm, the boy bishop anxious to show off his conquest, and to triumph over Tom to the very last.

Tom had brought a large bundle of his belongings. And Borghild, smiling slyly, also brought a large bundle, ostensibly for Jimmy. These were stowed into the cockpit of the plane.

The motor was started, the skids were removed, and Tom settled into the driver's seat.

Then Scarface stepped off to the edge of the crowd for a fond farewell embrace of Borghild.

At the same moment Helga and Astrid drew Nils one side.

"Let go of Theresa for a moment, if you can," they cajoled him. "We have an important secret for you—it concerns her."

Then, as they led him away from the crowd, the airplane motor gave an impatient roar behind them, as they bent near to whisper in his ear.

"I can't hear a word you say," exclaimed Nils a bit testily. "You'll have to speak a little louder."

"All right!" they shouted. "What we wanted to tell you was that Theresa's replacing Scarface and is eloping with Tom Jones in the plane!"

Nils wheeled.

The crowd was scattering as the plane soared from the field, sending up a cloud of red pollen. Then it sped away to the northward, with Tom and his eloping bride waving good-by to those below.

THE ELOPERS adjusted to their ears the phones installed long ago by Eric and Angus to make conversation possible above the roar of the motors. As the plateau city gradually faded behind them in the distance, Tom suggested:

"Let's land somewhere and have a real talk at last, dear."

So the amphibian plane volplaned down to the water, and then taxied up to the beach of a little island. Tom clambered out of the cockpit, and assisted the erstwhile tomboy to alight, which she did shyly, blushing.

The two sat down on the sand, nestling in each other's arms. Tom broke the silence to ask humbly, "How did you happen to pick me, when you could have become queen of all the center of the earth by marrying Nils Uppri? Is it just because you wouldn't marry a priest?"

"No," she replied, "I got over that idea long ago, for bishops are different down here, more like kings or congressmen or something, than like the bishops of my church. I don't know just why I didn't fall for Nils. We got along fine together in our log fort."

Tom glowered, but Theresa leaned over and kissed him, until he smiled again.

"You know, it's a funny thing," said she. "At first, I thought I cared for Nils; but after a while every time he would kiss me and put his arms around me, I'd shut my eyes and make believe it was you."

"I'd rather do it myself," interjected Tom, suiting the action to the word.

How these two flew out through the polar orifice of the earth, and down over the continent of Greenland in the dead darkness of polar winter, finally to crash off the coast of Nova Scotia, would take too long to tell. Suffice it to state that they lived through their hardships, reached Boston, and were duly married by a cardinal in person.

From them I learned this story, for they looked me up because of my having written up the earlier adventures of Eric and Angus.

They are now as happy as I would wish for them. The fly in the ointment is that none of Tom's Back Bay friends will believe his story of Chicago gangsters, the frozen north, and the land beyond the pole. They claim, these bluestockings, that it is all a mere yarn to cover up the bald fact that Tom has gone and married a little guttersnipe whom he picked up somehow during the summer—this in spite of the fact that the girl is rapidly developing into as fine a lady as one would care to know.

But they love each other devotedly, and may eventually live down the suspicions of his friends.

Incidentally, the little old ex-jockey, named Arty, was let onto the secret of their intended flight, and sent out a message by them. He wants the Sydney broadcasting station to use the Rogers underground aërial occasionally, so that he can try to tune in on them. Australian papers please copy.

ABOUT THE AUTHOR

THE IDENTITY OF Ralph Milne Farley is shrouded in mystery. When his first story, "The Radio Man," appeared in the *Argosy—All-Story Weekly*, in 1924, it was announced editorially that the author was the world's leading authority in two lines, to name either of which would be instantly to reveal his identity.

"The Radio Man" attracted considerable attention and comment in literary and technical circles, and one newspaper, the Boston *Post*, even put one of its best sleuth-hounds on the trail. By careful study of the internal evidence in the story, especially the fact that the narrative started on Chappaquiddick Island, off the coast of Massachusetts, and that the hero was described as a member of the Harvard class of 1909, the *Post* narrowed the field to two Harvard '09 men who own estates on the island in question: namely, Dr. Francis M. Rackermann and former State Senator Roger Sherman Hoar. Dr. Rackemann is a recognized authority on hay-fever and eczema; whereas Senator Hoar has written the outstanding American texts on "Constitutional Conventions" and on "Ballistics."

Recently apropos Farley's "The Radio Flyers," the Boston *Post* announced that further evidence, namely a similarity between certain passages in one of Farley's stories and a whimsy entitled "Blue Dandelions," published years ago by Senator Hoar in the *Atlantic Monthly*, definitely establishes their identity. The *Post* ought to know, as Hoar used to work for them.

So we are accepting this verdict, and are publishing the portrait of the Senator.

Hon. Roger Sherman Hoar (alias Ralph Milne Farley), was born in Waltham, Massachusetts, on April 8, 1887. Until eight years ago he lived in Concord, Massachusetts.

He holds three degrees from Harvard University. In addition to his service in the State Senate, he has been Assistant Attorney General of Massachusetts, and Legal Advisor of the

Ralph Milne Farley

Constitutional Convention of 1917. He resigned that position to enlist as a private at the outbreak of the World War. Rapidly rising to captain, he served as senior instructor in military surveying at the Coast Artillery School, and later on the Technical Staff.

After the war, Bucyrus Company, of South Milwaukee, Wisconsin, the largest manufacturer of excavating machinery in America, was looking for a combined lawyer and engineer to take charge of their legal affairs, and persuaded Captain Hoar to resign his commission. He is now the attorney of their successor, Bucyrus-Erie Company. On the side, he is Lecturer in Physics at Marquette University, and a reserve major of the Technical Staff of the United States Army.

Major Hoar is the author of a number of works on law and engineering, and is a contributor to legal and technical magazines.

He is the inventor of several patented devices," including the north-finding apparatus used by his hero, *Eric Redmond,* in

"The Radio Flyers." This is an actual practical instrument, useful in aiming big guns, the patent to which is owned by the War Department.

His chief interests, outside his official position, are his family, higher mathematics, blue dandelions and writing.

He is married, has a daughter and two sons, and lives in South Milwaukee.

Although each of his titles contains the word "Radio," he has never owned a radio set. No item of the technical background of any of his stories has ever been successfully challenged.

THE ARGOSY™ LIBRARY

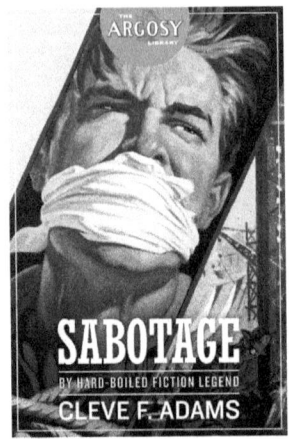

SABOTAGE
BY HARD-BOILED FICTION LEGEND
CLEVE F. ADAMS

CHAMPION OF LOST CAUSES
WILLIAM F. NOLAN
MAX BRAND

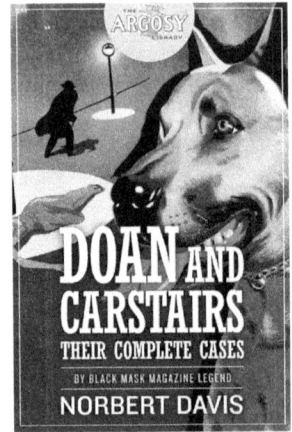

DOAN AND CARSTAIRS
THEIR COMPLETE CASES
BY BLACK MASK MAGAZINE LEGEND
NORBERT DAVIS

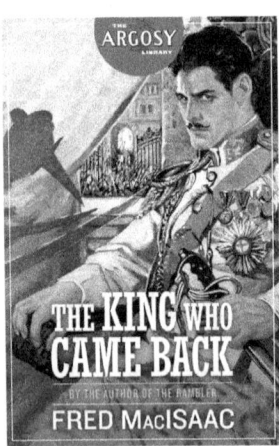

THE KING WHO CAME BACK
BY THE AUTHOR OF THE RAMBLER
FRED MacISAAC

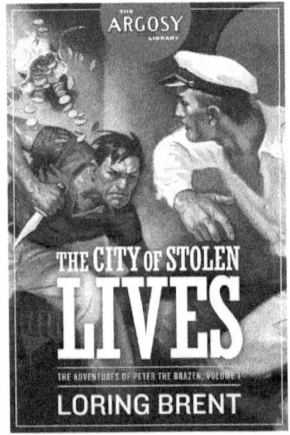

THE CITY OF STOLEN LIVES
THE ADVENTURES OF PETER THE BRAZEN, VOLUME I
LORING BRENT

THE RADIO GUN-RUNNERS
BY SCIENCE FICTION LEGEND
RALPH MILNE FARLEY

BLOOD RITUAL
THE ADVENTURES OF SCARLET AND BRADSHAW, VOLUME I
THEODORE ROSCOE

THE SCARLET BLADE
THE RAKEHELLY ADVENTURES OF CLEVE AND D'ENTREVILLE, VOLUME I
MURRAY R. MONTGOMERY

SEMI DUAL
THE COMPLETE CABALISTIC CASES OF
THE OCCULT DETECTIVE, VOLUME 2: 1912–13
J.U. GIESY AND JUNIUS B. SMITH

SOUTH OF FIFTY-THREE
BY THE AUTHOR OF THE TORCH
JACK BECHDOLT

SERIES 2 • AVAILABLE SPRING 2015

www.ingramcontent.com/pod-product-compliance
Lightning Source LLC
Chambersburg PA
CBHW051828020726
47502CB00005B/1691